THE DISAPPEARANCES

Also by Michael J. McCann

Twilight Road
In These Disconsolate Woods
Project Changeling
The Long Road Into Darkness
A Death in Winter
No Sadness of Farewell
Persistent Guilt
Burn Country
Sorrow Lake
The Rainy Day Killer
The Fregoli Delusion
Marcie's Murder
Blood Passage
The Ghost Man

THE DISAPPEARANCES

A Mark Heron Mystery

Michael J. McCann

The Plaid Raccoon Press
2023

THE DISAPPEARANCES

ISBN: 978-1-927884-28-7 (paperback)
    978-1-927884-29-4 (e-book)

Front cover image: Fahad bin Kamel Anik/Unsplash
Back cover image: Ysbrand Cosjin/Shutterstock
Author photo: Michael J. McCann
Book design & cover design: Michael J. McCann

Visit the author's website at www.mjmccann.com

To the memory of Leo Cullum, Charles Addams, Rowland Emett, Gahan Wilson, Bill Lee, George Booth, and all the other single-panel gag cartoonists who have entertained us throughout our lives.

CHAPTER

One

When I was a much younger man, I drew a cartoon for *Saturday Magazine* that generated a lot of response, both positive and negative, from their readership. In the cartoon, an old man sits in a rocking chair on his front porch with a shotgun across his knees. A Girl Guide holding a box of cookies looks up at him with wide eyes. The caption reads, "Get offa my property."

The cartoon ran with an article on the rising question of gun ownership in the nation and the controversy surrounding gun registration, which had popped out of the woodwork once again as a topic of discussion. I hadn't meant to take sides, though. I was merely trying to be funny.

Now that I'm an old man myself, enjoying the summer sunshine in a rocking chair on my own verandah, I often think of that cartoon and do my best to regard the traffic passing on the road in front of my place with benign indifference. Since no one stops other than the occasional courier, Canada Post, or someone using the driveway to turn around and reverse course, I don't really care who goes by.

Such was my mindset on this particular August afternoon. I sipped my bourbon, drew on my cigar, and only frowned slightly when a very noisy motorcycle approached on the road from the direction of town, slowed, and turned into my driveway.

I put my glass aside, stuck the cigar in the corner of my mouth, and waited. My driveway is fairly long, more than a hundred feet, and it's lined with mature blue spruce trees on either side, so it took a moment for me to see the bike, a Harley, as it pulled up behind my Escalade and shut down.

I watched the driver lower the kickstand, dismount, and use both hands to get free of the big black helmet. I was somewhat surprised when I saw that it was a young woman, shaking out shoulder-length black hair as she put the helmet on the seat of the bike and walked over.

"Are you Mark Heron?"

She wore a black leather jacket despite the warm air, blue jeans that had seen better days, and scuffed cowboy boots. Her hair was straight, with a slight wave at the ends, and it stuck across her forehead in damp spears.

"That would be me."

She took a folded newspaper out of her jacket pocket and held it up.

"Did you draw this?"

I leaned forward. I knew right away what she was referring to, but for whatever reason I decided to be a bit of a dickhead about it.

"I can't quite see it."

She thumped up the stairs and tossed the paper onto my lap.

I pulled out my reading glasses. It was a copy of this

week's *Sentinel*, which had published today and would be in my mailbox this evening along with a bunch of flyers and other junk delivered by someone who went door to door in a beat-up Toyota for the few bucks it paid them each week.

"Yep. This is mine."

It was an illustration of a young man with his head down and his hands folded between his knees. His hair was in disarray and his expression was sad, almost sorrowful. I'd sold it to Patrick for an article he was running on local homelessness. I turned to the editorial page where my weekly cartoon would also be printed, but she snatched the paper out of my hand before I had a chance to squint at it critically.

"Where is he? When did you last see him?"

"Who?"

"The guy, dammit. The guy."

"Nineteen ninety-one," I replied. "February."

"Fuck that. Couldn't have been more than a couple weeks ago. Stop lying and tell me where he is."

I took off my reading glasses. "I think we're talking at cross purposes, my dear. Who are you, by the way?"

CHAPTER

Two

Her name was Rosemary. Other details to follow, apparently. She didn't look to me like a Rosemary. She looked like someone you wouldn't want to cross. Her hazel eyes bore through me like angry lasers, and her fists, admittedly a typical size for a female her age, had prominent knuckles that would likely hurt quite a bit if they made contact with your jaw.

I invited her to sit down, but she ignored me.

Okay, then.

I explained the genesis of the drawing that had upset her.

In late February 1991, I was embedded with Canadian personnel setting up a field hospital at Al Qaysumah, Saudi Arabia, not long before the end of the Gulf War, in something they called "Operation Scalpel." The young man in question was a physician assigned to the hospital, Lieutenant Rod MacPherson. At the moment I'd sketched his portrait, he'd just finished examining a Kuwaiti orphan whose parents had been killed in the same explosion that had cost him three toes on his right foot. Dr. MacPherson sent him off to be prepped for surgery and took a moment to compose himself.

I drew the person I saw in front of me—young, frightened, appalled. Without acknowledging my presence, he slowly got to his feet and walked away. The sketch ended up in the files with all my other unsold work from that assignment.

I'd never been overseas before, let alone dropped into the middle of a desert war, and I was disoriented and upset the entire time I was there. I thought I could be another Bill Mauldin, the famous cartoonist whose work ran in *Stars and Stripes*, the U.S. Army publication, during World War Two, but it turned out to be a lot more difficult than I'd thought. I didn't handle the assignment very well.

Just the same, I was only thirty-seven and at the peak of my creative abilities, so I threw myself into my work and produced what I still believe was my best stuff ever, as far as both single-panel cartoons and illustrations were concerned. I went through about twenty sketch books and several packages of photocopy paper scrounged from hospital administrative staff before my time was up and they flew me home.

Looking at the material later, I could see that my style had quickly adapted to the emotional environment. Although Saudi Arabia itself was bright and hot, my drawings were dark and cold, sombre in tone with heavy chiaroscuro and thick lines. I was hardly a war correspondent, just a cartoon guy on a field trip to hell, and everything I drew reflected how much I hated and feared the place. The war correspondents I was embedded with seemed to take it all in stride and were matter-of-fact and businesslike about what we were seeing, hearing, and smelling, but I was of a different mentality, I guess, and I had a hard time adapting.

After returning home, I sold enough to Canadian Press and several different magazines to make a lot of money. While I was already well known in the cartooning world, it was definitely a career-making project. It also formed the basis of my second book, and even won me a Governor General's Award nine years later, shortly after the award for art and media was instituted, as belated acknowledgement of my accomplishments.

Nevertheless, I promised myself never to do that sort of thing again, and by God I didn't. It took me almost a year to get over the after-effects. I was afraid I'd developed post-traumatic stress disorder, but eventually I slid back into my old, easy-going, humorous self again, thank the gods above, and life continued onward.

I explained this to Rosemary as simply as I could, leaving out most of the details, including the award and the PTSD stuff. When Patrick asked for something to accompany his article, I told her, I'd thought of this drawing right away. It had stayed in the filing cabinet too long, and here was an opportunity for it to speak out on an important, if unrelated, social problem.

She didn't bother to hide her disappointment.

"Shit. So it's not Nathan. That's what you're saying?"

"His name was Dr. Roderick MacPherson."

"Shit."

"Why don't you tell me what this is all about?"

"Damn. You wouldn't be interested. You're just some old retired artist guy."

I smiled. Sticks and stones. Holding up my cigar, I said, "Is the smoke bothering you?"

Instead of answering, she sat down and pulled out a pack of cigarettes. I passed her my lighter. She used it and gave it back.

"My friend Grace's cousin disappeared almost two months ago," she said, exhaling smoke. "Nathan Notwell. Right in town. Some people call him Nathan Nothing. He's twenty-seven but mentally disabled. Brain damage from a car accident. He was walking home from work. Somebody saw him in the park a couple of blocks from his place, then zip. Gone. Vanished."

"I'm sorry to hear that," I said, meaning it. "What about the police?"

"They searched for him, had a thing on Crime Stoppers and all the rest of it. Nothing. He can't get along on his own. That's why Grace took him in after the accident." She tapped her cigarette. "So when I saw the drawing, I called the paper from work and found out you did it. It looks just like him."

"I'm sorry."

She stared at her cigarette, then glanced over her shoulder at the front door. "Where's your wife?"

"Connecticut, I think. Or maybe it's Arizona now. I'm not sure."

"Divorced, eh?"

"Yep. Thirty-seven years last March."

She flicked her cigarette out onto the lawn and stood up. "Sorry to bother you."

"No bother at all. I just wish there was something I could do to help."

"Sure. Whatever."

"No, I mean it."

"Screw it, pal. Forget it."

She clumped back down the stairs without another word. Settling the helmet back on her head, she gunned the bike and drove away.

CHAPTER

Three

Long after the sound of her engine had faded away in the direction of town, I could still feel her anger and disappointment hanging in the air like a lingering vapour. I felt bad for her, and I felt bad that someone had disappeared, but if the police couldn't find him, I wasn't sure what I could do to help.

I walked down the driveway to check the mailbox. A vehicle passed on the road, their muffler badly in need of replacement, but I couldn't see them through the blue spruces. Noisy day today, it would seem.

The weekly paper and flyers weren't there yet, but Canada Post had delivered a cheque. It was from one of the magazines that required an American bank account, which I didn't have, in order to set up direct deposit. Several of the publications that bought my stuff operated this way, but I didn't really care. If they wanted to continue incurring the expense of cutting a physical cheque and mailing it out to me, rather than jig their system to accommodate Canadian banks, that was up to them.

As I walked back to the house I remembered, as I always

did, the border collie who'd passed away at my feet while I was eating my Easter Sunday dinner a year ago. Cody was a very bright dog with a better vocabulary than the guy who fixed my car. I'd open the front door and say, "Let's go check the mail," and he'd trot down the driveway ahead of me and sit a safe distance away from the edge of the road as I took out whatever was in the box. Then he'd lead the way back to the house. I thought of him every time I went down to check the mail, and I knew I'd never stop missing him.

I thought constantly about getting another dog, but I didn't think it would be fair to the animal, who might actually outlive me this time, and then where would we be? I turned seventy next month and probably had about ten or twelve good years left until something needed to be done as far as assisted living or long-term care was concerned, and I didn't want to take a chance that the dog would have to be placed with new owners while passing inevitably into his own dotage.

Better to tough it out on my own.

Back in the house, I tossed the cheque on the hall table and grabbed a beer from the refrigerator. There was still time left in the day to get a little work done, but I took the beer into the solarium instead and sank down into my recliner.

This thing about turning seventy had given me a case of the yips. Granted it was only a number, duration measured in years and days and hours and seconds, and as such was more illusion than reality, at least according to many physicists and deep thinkers I'd read about in magazines that also carried my work. It may feel real to us in a psychological way, they maintained, but it wasn't a part of fundamental reality.

Okay, but even more important than the number was the state of my health, wouldn't you think? I took medication for my blood sugar, blood pressure, and cholesterol levels, all of which stayed within a range that kept my doctor happy. My teeth were in good shape and my weight was ballpark appropriate for my height. I went through a brief routine of light exercises in the morning and I also went for walks, so there wasn't really much to worry about right now, was there?

And most importantly, my right hand remained steady and without tremors, so I could still draw the way I've always drawn, casually and with confidence.

Just the same, I'd been feeling a little vulnerable lately, if that's the right word to use. Memento mori, an awareness of one's impending death, stirred in my fretting brain at the slightest of associations, such as a lost man who was possibly dead by now. Or a birthday I was dreading, because I didn't know how many more I'd have left after that.

I sipped my beer and forced a smile at the setting sun, its glare dimmed through the special-grade solarium glass that had cost so much to install. In my profession, there were any number of ways to approach the subject. There were grim reaper cartoons, firing squad cartoons, graveyard cartoons, hospital room cartoons, Pearly Gates cartoons—you name it. I myself was responsible for a number of them over the years, including one of an old man on his deathbed speaking to his dirt-covered son: "When you searched the garden for the loot I didn't hide, did you find out where I lost my dentures?" Not good, but hey. It sold.

We dealt with the fear of death by laughing at it. Making fun of it. Ridiculing it.

Gallows humour. Black comedy. A gag featuring a lane into a cemetery with a Dead End sign at the entrance.

I grabbed a sketchbook I kept next to the recliner and flipped to a blank page.

Two middle-aged women standing in front of a headstone in a cemetery. The caption reads: "He forgot to tell me which suit he wanted, so I gave them that awful plaid jacket. It gave me the creeps every time I looked in the closet."

CHAPTER

Four

Rosemary's visit, and the story of Nathan Notwell's disappearance, bothered me throughout the next day. I went for my daily walk and the missing man followed me, into the woods and all the way back to the fallen tree where I liked to rest for a moment and hydrate before returning to the house.

I hadn't read about it in the newspaper, although Patrick must have covered it. I didn't read much of anything he published other than the regular bird column, so whatever he'd run, I'd missed it. Such a terrible thing to have happened. Worst of all, as I said, I knew that after this much time had passed, the chances that the man was still alive had diminished significantly.

I drank and spat, drank and swallowed, and stared at the shadows of the abandoned house that was visible through the trees on the lot behind mine. As always, it gave me the willies, so I turned my back on it again and drank more water, trying to think of nothing in particular for the next few minutes.

Pulling out a handkerchief, I wiped stray droplets of

water from my beard, mopped the sweat from my forehead, and headed back.

My property was ten acres in size, the rest of the former farm having been subdivided from the house after I acquired it and sold to a local farmer looking for extra acreage to grow hay as a cash crop. I maintained a walking path around the perimeter of what still belonged to me, and the circuit provided good exercise and a chance to clear the cobwebs from my head.

Once I got back to the house, I showered and ate lunch. Then it was into the studio to get some work done.

Cartoonists work in different ways, and various publications have their own preferences when it comes to the submission process. A few still favour physical submissions, which normally involve a batch of ten roughs on eight-and-a-half by eleven paper, mailed flat with a cardboard stiffener and a self-addressed, stamped envelope for returns.

Others prefer digital submissions. Some look for the batch to be merged into a single PDF file while others want JPG files of each individual rough. Ferd Johnson, the creator of Moon Mullins, once said that a cartoonist could work wherever there's a mailbox. Today, this truism also extended to an Inbox in an e-mail account. I really didn't have a preference one way or the other, since I had a physical mailbox, which I've mentioned already, as well as a Mac Pro with a very expensive printer/scanner to handle the digital side of things.

Once the batch went in, the editor looked through the roughs and (hopefully) made a note of the ones they wanted to buy. The batch came back and I got to work on the final versions of the chosen few.

Again, every cartoonist had their own way of doing

things, but for roughs I usually preferred to start with a light sketch in pencil, which I'd follow up with a grease pencil (a.k.a. china marker) to put down the firm lines. I drew my roughs usually while working from something in a sketchbook I'd dashed off at one point or another beforehand. Sketchbooks were for ideas, not fine art. Ideas were difficult enough to come by without fretting over style and textures and shadows and so on right at the beginning of the process.

Get the idea down; get it into the studio; get it into a rough.

It was already the second week in August, and I'd received a batch of returned Halloween gags from which three had been purchased. My next job, as I explained, was to produce the finished versions and get them back in as soon as possible.

For this particular magazine I preferred to submit wash drawings as a final product. After transferring the rough drawing to a piece of paper heavy enough to take the wash without wrinkling or bubbling, I went over the pencil lines with India ink to finalize the outlines. Once the ink was dry, it was time for the wash part. These gags would have two different shades of grey shadows, so I'd created two pools of diluted ink, one light and one darker, and I'd already applied the lighter shading. Now that it was dry, it was time to put down the darker wash and let *it* dry.

This technique might seem a little labour-intensive, but it had been favoured by such greats as Peter Arno and Charles Addams for their gag cartoons in *The New Yorker*, and I'd adapted it as the best way to go when selling to that esteemed publication.

So I went into the studio, arranged the three roughs on my work table, and took one over to the drawing table.

As I was applying the dark wash, my mind was still on the missing man. Nathan Nothing. I could imagine how traumatized his cousin would be. I stopped and looked at what I was working on. Two costumed children stood on the sidewalk looking into their goody bags. It was a two-line gag. One child was saying, "I got another apple. What'd you get?" The second child replies, "Broccoli. Health nuts just don't get it, do they?"

I messed up the dark wash, smearing it into the second boy's goody bag, so I stood up, turned off the lights, and went into the kitchen. I knew from long experience that when I didn't have it, I didn't have it. Retreat and live to draw another day.

I decided I should probably drive into town to pick up a few things at the grocery store, as something completely different to do. Since I loved to cook, food was another little world in which I could lose myself for a short while.

I grabbed my shopping list off the refrigerator door and headed out.

Prices at the grocery store where I normally shopped had gone through the roof as post-pandemic inflation swept through the country, making it difficult to stay within a reasonable budget while buying enough to put decent meals on the table, so I'd recently switched to the other big store in town. The prices there were a little lower, enough to make a difference, and the selection was better.

I dawdled in the produce section, picking up a few fresh items for salads and bagging some fruit and vegetable items. If I restocked on pasta and fish, and bought the makings for a nice oily moussaka, I thought I could make several meals that would last through the weekend and on into early next week.

As I browsed, I passed a woman and her young son

who were looking at the fruit. There wasn't much in her cart, and if I judged by the poor state of their clothing and footwear, their food budget was likely very low.

I heard the boy ask if they could get some apples. I saw her look at the price and shake her head.

"We can't afford them right now."

I thought of the apple trees on my property that gave me the gift of their bounty every other summer, and I bit my lip. When they'd moved out of the way, I grabbed a bag and dropped in half a dozen good-looking specimens, thinking about a piece Patrick had run in the *Sentinel* a month or so ago on food insecurity. (Yes, I'd actually read it.) I knew I'd witnessed an example of exactly what he'd been writing about.

Leaving produce, I turned into the next aisle, where the condiments, pickles, and barbecue sauces were stocked. As I did so, I glanced over at the express checkout on my left and was startled to see Rosemary standing there, working cash. I hesitated for a moment, thinking it through, and then left my cart and joined the line-up with the bag of apples in hand. When my turn came, I watched her ring them up and I paid for them with my debit card.

"I've been thinking about things," I said as she handed me the receipt. "Maybe we can talk some more about Nathan."

She said nothing, looking past me for the next customer. Unfortunately for her, we were momentarily alone.

"Maybe there's something I could do to help after all," I said, picking up the bag of apples.

"Fuck off."

"I'm sorry?"

"I don't need the help of some useless geezer, so just fucking forget about it."

"Why are you so angry with me?"

"You're holding up the line."

I looked behind me and, sure enough, someone had come up with a hand basket filled with bags of ketchup-flavoured potato chips. Tail between my legs, I went back to my cart and resumed shopping.

A few aisles later I passed the woman and her boy. Pausing, I put the apples into her cart and handed her the receipt.

"They're paid for."

She stared at me for a moment, frowning, then put the apples back in my cart and dropped in the receipt. "No, thanks. I don't know you. Thanks anyway."

She wheeled off and disappeared around the corner at the end of the aisle.

I guess I wasn't very good at helping people.

When my shopping was done, I lined up at the checkout lane farthest from express, and I tried not to swallow my tongue at the final total owing from my cartful of items. Prices had gone up again here, as well.

After bagging my purchases, I wheeled the cart down toward the exit. Involuntarily my eyes went over to the express lane and locked with Rosemary's.

She flipped me the bird.

I left the store in a hurry.

CHAPTER

Five

My idea of a fun time on a Friday evening was to have dinner at the McDonald's in town and hang around afterward with a cup of coffee and a small, unobtrusive sketchbook I kept in the Escalade for the occasion. It was a very busy time for the restaurant, with a lot of people coming and going, and it gave me a chance to catch up on my people-sketching.

As usual, there was a mix of customers. I sketched a couple of young men, likely single, dressed in messy work clothes and steel-toed boots. They seldom sat down in the lobby to eat, preferring to take their food out with them, either to eat in their truck or at home with a beer. Also common were family groups, mom and dad with small children. Mom's night out; a break from fixing supper.

There were a few elderly folks, almost all of whom ate inside where I could surreptitiously sketch them. Usually they were couples I'd seen before, out on a date night. They seldom spoke, concentrating on their food, but always seemed comfortable and at ease with each other.

I tried not to let people know I was drawing them. Once,

in my younger days, I was sketching some guy in a bar and he took exception to it. Mind you, we'd both had one too many, but I still don't think there was any reason for him to have broken my nose. If you look closely, you can see it's a little flatter than normal. Anyway, after that I took care not to tip my hand, so to speak.

The way I worked it was to observe a person for a few moments, as long as I could get away with, and then dash off a sketch without looking back at them. That way, I hoped, it would appear that I was putting something down on paper that had nothing to do with them. Glancing up and down, up and down, would be a dead giveaway and might just land me in hot water. Again.

I was busily drawing away, eyes down, when someone stopped at my table.

I looked up.

"I thought it was you," she said.

"Hi, Rosemary." I put down my pencil.

"Look, I'm sorry for being bitchy." She still wore her green polo shirt and black trousers from work, and was apparently picking up her supper to eat at home, like the single males I mentioned before.

"That's all right."

"No, it's not. Anyway, I have to go home, but I'll drop by your place in an hour or so."

"Sure. Sounds fine to me."

She left my table and went out the back door.

I exhaled slowly, closing my sketchbook.

She was a reasonably attractive young woman, and she'd pinned her hair up in back for work, but even without her leather jacket and torn jeans she exuded a toughness that was impossible to overlook.

Standing up, I heard a Harley engine outside roaring

from the parking lot and felt slightly relieved that I could make it to the Escalade without encountering her again.

CHAPTER

Six

I was back out on my verandah watching the sun work its way down toward the treeline, puffing on a cigar. I preferred petit coronas, about four and a half inches long, usually an Arturo Fuente Don Carlos from the Dominican Republic. A fourteen-dollar cigar, but a very pleasant and relaxing smoke.

At the moment, Tennyson Road was quiet. One of the things I loved about the place was the amazing number of birds that lived in the trees around the house. Not long ago I downloaded an app to my cellphone that can identify them by song, and over the summer I'd recorded a number of birds I had no idea lived in the same habitat as I did.

The blue spruce trees along the driveway were popular with song sparrows and a family of cardinals that had built their nest deep in the prickly boughs to raise their young. Elsewhere around the house, the maple, birch, and cedar trees hosted everything from nuthatches and chickadees to red-eyed vireos, ovenbirds, rose-breasted grosbeaks, great crested flycatchers, flickers, and mourning doves.

Some of these birds I'd never seen before with the naked

eye, but I'd heard them chattering away in the tree canopy without knowing what they were. The app was busily educating me on the identity of my feathered neighbours. It was wonderful.

There was the vireo now. No, that was the rose-breasted grosbeak, wasn't it?

I was still pretty much a tyro at this stuff, and the cellphone was in the kitchen.

Before long the ambience was broken by the deep-throated grumbling of a Harley-Davidson slowing down and turning into my driveway.

This time she sat on the top step with her back against the railing post, one knee drawn up and the other leg straight out. Her hair was tied back with a red paisley bandanna, and her jeans were split at the knees. Under her leather jacket she wore a T-shirt with a possum on it. The caption said, "Live Weird: Fake Your Death".

Maybe, just maybe, I thought, this young lady could learn to appreciate my own offbeat sense of humour.

I offered her a drink, and she asked for a Coke.

"I don't touch booze," she said.

I brought her out a cold can and a glass, along with a glass of bourbon for myself. She popped the tab and guzzled without bothering with the glass.

"No drugs, either, in case you're wondering. None of that shit."

"Good to know." I sat down and sipped my bourbon.

"He's an odd sort of guy," she said without preamble. "Very quiet and shy."

I nodded, watching her pull out her cigarettes and fire one up. I set my ashtray down next to her foot, and she tapped into it.

"He's twenty-seven, like I said before. The accident

happened three years ago. He was going to the Athens Cornfest with his parents. His dad was driving, his mom was up front, and he was in back. His girlfriend at the time couldn't go with them because she had to work."

She drew heavily and exhaled. "They were hit head-on by some kid trying to pass a moving van. Both of his parents were killed instantly, and Nathan had really bad head injuries. Ended up with brain damage and was in the hospital for two months. Eventually he could talk again and do basic stuff like addition and subtraction, tell the time, or read a kids' storybook. Other than that, he was pretty helpless. Grace took him in out of the goodness of her heart, but he turned out to be a real darling and they all love him."

"Excuse me for a second." I got up and went into the house. I grabbed a sketchbook and pencil and brought them out with me.

She watched me flip to a fresh page and start drawing. "He can have a decent conversation with you."

"I see."

"Yeah. He likes watching sports on TV and can follow the teams. He's a Leafs fan and loves the Blue Jays. He can't drink because of all the meds he has to take, so he scarfs a lot of Coke. Like me, I guess. Works at a woollen mill on the river. Walks there and back home, even in winter. He always walks down Pine Street to the park and hangs around there for a while before going home. One of his co-workers told police he drove by the park on the way home and saw him sitting on a bench. After that, zip."

My hand flew over the page. I was sketching Dr. MacPherson from memory, and since my memory was still excellent, thank you very much, it was a good likeness.

I turned the sketchbook around.

She stared for a moment through a veil of cigarette smoke. "Not bad. His eyes are closer together. And not as round."

I pulled an eraser from my pocket, one of the white plastic kinds, and made the changes.

"Better. That's him. You're good."

"Thank you. Has Grace talked to the police lately?"

"Day before yesterday. There's another guy working on it now, or at least he has the file folder sitting on his desk. He told her he was sorry, but there's nothing new. That's partly why I decided to look you up."

"Even though I am a fucking useless geezer." I began to sketch her, sitting there with the cigarette held close to her ear, tufts of black hair sticking out from under the bandanna, eyes staring past me at nothing in particular.

"Yeah. I said I was sorry."

"You did." I flipped the page and started another one. "Maybe we should take a run in to the park, look around, see if something stands out."

She pointed her cigarette at me. "Now you're talking, mister."

"You know, you can call me Mark if you like."

"Sure."

"And I'll call you Rosemary. What's your last name, Rosemary?"

"Nolan." She stubbed out her cigarette. "Let's roll."

I closed my sketchbook. "I was thinking more along the lines of tomorrow morning sometime."

"Christ." She got to her feet. "You old coots are all alike. Gotta stop and catch your breath every five minutes or you'll die of a heart attack. Just how old are you, anyways? A hundred?"

"Sixty-nine," I replied, with all the dignity I could

muster. "I won't be seventy until next month. How about you, my dear? Pushing twenty, are we?"

"Twenty-two, not that it's any of your damned business. What time do you crawl out of your coffin, Mark? Should I find something to do until eleven or so?"

"Nine thirty will be fine."

She clumped down the stairs. "See you then."

"Drive safely," I said.

CHAPTER

Seven

Rosemary rolled into the yard a few minutes before nine, but I was already out on the verandah, waiting for her.

Smart ass.

She told me to hop onto the back of her bike, which I thought was amusing, and she rolled her eyes when I opened the passenger door of the Escalade for her.

She seemed to be in a little better mood this morning, watching the scenery pass with an expression that lacked its usual pugnacity.

"So, where do you live, Rosemary Nolan?"

She chewed the corner of her lip for a moment and then released it so it could turn up into a little smile. "Wild Life Road. Just off Otty Lake Road. Know where that is?"

"Not exactly."

She shrugged.

I said, "No ring on your finger, so, not married yet. Living with your boyfriend?"

The smile quickly morphed into a frown. "What the hell."

"We've already discussed my marital status," I said mildly, "and that wasn't very traumatic."

She sighed theatrically. "No boyfriend. Rosie lives alone. Satisfied?"

"Sure."

As we approached the edge of town, she sighed again. "I live in a trailer at my cousin's place. In front of his house. He has a garage across the road. He fixes bikes."

"Like yours?"

"Like mine."

I slowed for a traffic light that was about to turn red.

"It's nice enough," she said. "My trailer. I fixed it up pretty good. I don't need a lot of stuff, so. . . ."

"It sounds comfortable."

"Yeah. Bryan's a decent guy. His house is so-so; he spent his money on setting up the shop. Anyway, his wife is nice and his kids are the greatest."

I was slightly amazed to be getting this much information out of her.

She directed me to the park, which was at the far end of town. Centennial Park was an expanse of grass on Pine Street between Brock and Cockburn Streets. It took up the front half of the block. A fountain in a dry, circular cement pool occupied the middle, perhaps another centennial project now showing its age. It had been built when Mike Pearson was prime minister, one of the many projects undertaken to commemorate the hundredth year of Confederation. The grass was kept trimmed by the town, and there were a couple of nice gardens with perennials and flowering shrubs, so I could see why Nathan found it a calming and pleasant place to linger on his way home from work.

It was a residential neighbourhood, a mixture of wartime bungalows on one side of the street and brick houses with big front lawns on the other. Mature maples and elm trees lined the boulevards on either side. It was quiet. I saw a few cars and pickup trucks parked in driveways, automatic sprinklers watering lawns, cats curled up on verandahs, flowers in gardens.

Slipping my knapsack from my shoulder, I took out my sketchbook and artist box, sat down on a bench, and began to draw.

Rosemary watched me for a few moments, arms folded, before letting loose one of her drawn-out sighs. I was beginning to recognize them as a trademark expression.

"Why don't you just take pictures instead of wasting time with that?"

"For one thing," I replied, pencil flying across the paper, "my cellphone's charging in the kitchen, where it belongs. For another thing, this is what I do. It's how I'm wired. I see things differently this way. Notice details I might not, otherwise."

"Christ." She pulled out her own phone and started snapping.

"Don't worry," I told her, "I work quickly."

Was this the bench Nathan liked to sit on? Was he just relaxing and clearing his poor, tortured mind, or did he dread going home for some reason?

"Did he get along okay at home?" I asked, without looking up from what I was doing. "How was he with Grace and her kids?"

Rosemary sat down beside me. "Really good. The kids love him. He's like their big brother. And once he settled down, he was no trouble for Grace at all. Liked to help her around the house and look after the kids when he was off and she was at work."

I turned the page and started another sketch, looking in a different direction.

A woman appeared at the far intersection, walking an Airedale on a leash. She and the dog crossed the street and made their way along the far edge of the park. I included them in my sketch as they slowly disappeared from sight.

"Ellison, the co-worker, saw him here," Rosemary said. "In the park. Then he was gone."

I sighed before realizing I was starting to sound like her. I closed my sketchbook and gathered up my things.

"We should talk to Grace now."

CHAPTER

Eight

Grace Notwell lived in a run-down, two-storey tenement on a street two blocks from the park. A beat-up Ford Fiesta sat in the scrap of driveway, adding further particles of rust to the atmosphere with each tick of the clock, so I parked at the curb in front.

When Grace opened the door, I could smell the unmistakable odours of poverty—stale perspiration, the lingering scent of cooked food, unwashed laundry, cat litter, and other unidentifiables.

She waved us inside. Rosemary took the lead, hugging her friend and rubbing her back sympathetically as they moved down the hall to the living room. I hung back, the stranger, until they'd settled in chairs and Rosemary had waved off an offer of coffee. I looked around at the mess, saw no other place to sit, and propped my shoulder against the door jamb.

"This is Mark Heron," Rosemary said. "He's helping me look for Nathan."

Grace nodded, running her hands through her straight red hair. "Appreciate it." She said it while staring at the floor. There probably wasn't going to be a lot of eye contact, I realized.

"Where are the kids?"

"Annie's out with her friends. Grace Ellen's up in her room, like always. Bobby's playing soccer with his team."

It was like a status report, as though Grace monitored their whereabouts around the clock and Rosemary checked in on a regular basis to make sure everything was all right. Which was probably pretty close to the truth.

"We'll find him," Rosemary said. "We will. He's all right."

Grace said nothing, eyes still down.

"He wouldn't have just wandered off, would he?" I asked, a question that had been lingering at the back of my head all along.

Rosemary shot me a look. Grace merely shook her head. "No."

"He was slow," Rosemary said, "but he had his self-awareness and knew how to get home. He never got lost."

"Has he . . . been away from home like this before?"

"No."

"He's a very timid soul," Rosemary said. "He's very dependent on Grace."

"Please." Grace rubbed her face with her hands. "This isn't helping."

"We'll find him," Rosemary repeated.

After a moment, Grace looked up. She seemed to have cried all the tears she was going to cry some time ago, and now there was only a blankness in her eyes.

"I appreciate it, Rosie. I really do. But he's gone. There's nothing I can do about it."

"Don't say that! We'll keep looking. He's out there somewhere, waiting for us."

Grace shook her head. "It's too late. I've got to stop getting my hopes up. Can't you understand that?"

"Gracie . . ."

"You're a good friend. I really appreciate what you're trying to do. But it's just like that woman who disappeared in the spring. They never found her, either."

I frowned. "What woman?"

"What woman?" Rosemary echoed.

Grace rubbed her face with her hands. "It doesn't matter," she muttered. "If the police can't find them, there's nothing we can do. Nathan's gone. I have to accept that and move on. The same with the kids. They know they'll never see him again."

"That's not true," Rosemary insisted. "Not true."

I caught her eye and shook my head. To Grace I said, "We've bothered you enough this morning. Let's go, Rosemary."

I stood up. Rosemary made a face, then reached out and took her friend's hands. "Be strong, dear. Be strong."

"Yes."

Out in the car, Rosemary pounded the dashboard. "I can't believe it! She's given up. It's not right."

"She needs her space. We have no idea what she's been going through. She obviously feels complete responsibility for his disappearance. We've got to respect her need to work through the horror in her own way."

"Damn. Shit. Fuck."

As we sat there, a girl rode up on a bicycle and chained it to the metal electrical conduit running up the side of the house. Her straight red hair was similar to her mother's, only longer. She was in her early teens.

"Annie," Rosemary said, getting out.

I followed.

"Have you heard anything about Nathan?" Rosemary positioned herself between the girl and the little cement sidewalk leading to the front porch.

She shook her head and looked at me. "Who are you?"

"My name's Mark Heron," I said. "You're Annie?"

"Yeah."

"Mr. Heron's trying to help me find Nathan," Rosemary put in.

Annie said nothing to this. I could see the same blankness in her eyes that I'd seen in her mother's.

"Does Nathan have friends?" I asked. "Who might know something?"

"Not really. He was pretty much a loner. He didn't have friends."

"None at all? No one he spent time with on off days?"

Her posture shifted. "Renata, I guess."

I looked at Rosemary, who was frowning.

"Who's that?" she demanded. "Never heard of this person before."

Annie shrugged. "Moved here last year. Her mother works in the county office."

"What's her last name?"

"Um, I don't know. Wait, yeah. Bazuski. People call her Bazooka. She gets bullied a lot."

"Nice." Rosemary's hands went to her hips. "Where's she live? I want to talk to her."

"I don't know. Can I go in now? My bladder's about to explode."

"Sure."

She trotted around Rosemary and disappeared inside.

Back in the car, Rosemary massaged a fist in her hand. "We have to find this Bazuski woman."

"Yeah." I started the car. "Make some calls."

CHAPTER

Nine

The Bazuski family lived in a two-storey brick house on Maple Street, a block away from the river. The front lawn was a bit overgrown, and the driveway at the side led to a garage that looked like it needed a new door.

As we went up on the verandah and rang the bell, I looked at a pile of lumber and scattered building supplies. It seemed as though someone was making an effort to fix things up. As we waited, I could hear a hammer pounding away in the back yard. Someone cursed, and the pounding resumed.

A little dog barked somewhere in the house and then stopped.

The front door opened and a woman looked out at us.

"Mrs. Bazuski?" Rosemary had been elected as the person asking the questions this time. She'd made contact over the phone and arranged the time for the visit, so it was her voice that was familiar.

"Iona." Opening the door, she led us down the hallway into the dining room, where she sat down in front of her half-finished lunch. "Sorry, I'm diabetic, so I eat at set times. Can I get you something?"

"No, it's all right," Rosemary said, adopting a normal, friendly voice for once.

I sat down across the table from Iona, but she threw me a quick look. "Not there. That's Renata's place."

"Sorry." I got up and moved to the chair at the end of the table.

"We just wanted to speak to her for a minute," Rosemary said. "If that's okay."

"Sure, she's out the back right now, watching Darren. He's repairing the garage."

"We heard him," I said, trying to be friendly.

"I'll bet you did. Anyway, they say that a carpenter's house is always the very last one to get fixed up, so I'm glad at least he's spending some time out there today. You can see how much work this place needs."

"You should have a Hi's job jar."

"A what?"

"Hi's job jar."

She forked salad into her mouth and chewed.

"From the cartoon strip. *Hi and Lois*," I plunged on. "By Mort Walker and Dik Browne. Hi had so much to do around the house, Lois wrote down each job on a piece of paper and put it in a jar. The idea was that he'd pick something every Saturday to get done during the weekend. Hi's job jar."

Silence, other than the sound of Iona chewing and Rosemary grinding her teeth.

"Sorry."

Iona swallowed and directed her gaze at Rosemary. "Anyway, I'll talk to Renata with you. She doesn't do well with strangers because of social anxiety, but it'll be okay if I talk to her and you're here listening. She's fine with that.

If she gets anxious, I'll bring her Yorkie in. Butterscotch. Her companion dog. Renata's devoted to her."

"Sure," Rosemary said. "Okay."

"She's a slow learner," Iona said, examining a spinach leaf on the end of her fork. "The county has a community services program for adults with developmental disabilities. The objective is to help them live on their own, but Renata's a long way away from that. She's twenty-three, but functions at the level of a ten-year-old. She has a moderate form of PKU, phenylketonuria. Plus the epilepsy that goes with it. She belongs to a group that spends the day at the community centre twice a week learning life skills and socializing with others. That's where she met Nathan Notwell. They're friends."

She added other greens to the spinach leaf and shoved it in her mouth.

We waited politely for her to continue.

"I'm a civil planner," she said after washing down the greens with water. "I was hired by the county through a competitive process to manage the planning department. Double what I was making in Fredericton, although this place cost more, believe it or not, than what we got for selling our house back home."

She stood, gathering up her dishes. "I'll bring her in and have a little talk with her. You want to know about Nathan, how they got along, if he had other friends, that sort of thing."

"Yes."

When we were alone in the room, Rosemary gave me a fierce look. "Keep your yap buttoned, will you? *Hi and Lois*, for chrissakes. You're not helping any."

"Isn't this elder abuse or something?"

"You'll find out—" She broke off as we heard a door

opening and closing in the next room, which presumably was the kitchen. After a moment, Iona and her daughter came into the dining room. When the young woman hesitated, her mother gently guided her around the table on Rosemary's side to her place across from Iona.

When everyone was settled, Iona smiled at her daughter. "This is Rosemary. This is her friend, Mr. Heron. They're here to visit me. I'd like to talk to you about Nathan. Okay?"

"Yeah, okay. Nathan went away." She was small for her age, and very pale. Her straight, sand-coloured hair hung to her shoulders. She kept her eyes on her mother, not acknowledging either Rosemary or myself. She kept her hands folded on the table in front of her, but I could see her squeezing them together rhythmically as she tried to keep her stress under control.

I felt like I should get up and go. Leave this poor young woman alone. My heart went out to her and her mother.

"Yes, he did go away. We haven't really talked about this before, sweetheart, but I'm wondering if you know where he went."

"No. He stopped coming to the centre, and he stopped coming over to play."

"Does Nathan have other friends at the centre besides you, dear?"

"No. The others didn't like him. Like they don't like me. That's why we were friends, because nobody else would be."

I noticed she was referring to Nathan in the past tense. Perhaps she sensed something permanent about his disappearance.

Iona thought for a moment. "When your father would pick you up at the end of the day, did someone pick Nathan up, too?"

"No. He walked home. I wish I could do that."

"But we live a few blocks further away than he does, so your father wants to make sure you get home okay. Did Nathan always go home the same way?"

"I don't know. He talked about the park that he liked to go to and sit for a while before going home. He said it helped take his mind off things. He could stop being Nathan Nothing and go back to being Nathan Notwell for a little while. That's what the others called him at the centre. Nathan Nothing."

Iona poked her tongue into her cheek. "Hmm." To Rosemary she said, "If you want, we can talk about her friendship with Nathan a little more, to get a sense of what he was like around her. Would that be helpful? Address yourself to me, please."

"Yes," Rosemary said. "It would."

Iona nodded and smiled again at her daughter. "You like it when Nathan comes around to visit on Saturdays, don't you, dear?"

Renata nodded. "Even though he sometimes paid more attention to Butterscotch than me."

"Yes, we talked about that. He loves her, and his cousin won't let him have a dog."

"Yes. He liked to play catch with her. Throw her the ball and watch her fetch it." She shrugged. "I like it, too."

"What else would you guys do?"

Renata hesitated. "Things."

"What kind of things?"

"Sometimes we went for a walk."

"Oh?"

"When you're not here and Dad's watching me."

"Where would you go for a walk?"

"Sometimes to the park. We'd sit on his favourite bench and watch the cars go by."

"I see." The park was three blocks from their house. Apparently outside of Iona's comfort zone.

There was more, though. I watched Iona's tongue poking at the inside of her cheek again.

"Sometimes . . ."

"Yes?"

"He wanted to go down to the river."

"But you didn't, right? You're not allowed."

"Well . . ." Her eyes dropped.

I saw Iona's mouth work: *Fuck*. I figured that Darren was probably going to catch a boatload of shit when we left.

"I didn't want to, but he was going to go anyway and I still wanted to, you know, hang around with him, so I went, too."

"It's dangerous, Renata."

"No, it was okay. We'd just walk along the edge and I'd watch him throw stones in the water. I found some shells. Nathan said they were clam shells left by an otter after its lunch. They're in my room. In a box."

"Please don't go down there again."

"I won't. There's an old man who lives down there. Nathan said he's okay, but he scared me. I didn't like him being there."

I looked at Rosemary, startled. She looked at Iona.

Iona said, "What old man?"

CHAPTER

Ten

The river that snaked its way through town was a tributary of the Rideau. The water didn't look too bad, to my untrained eye, not overly dark or a weird colour or littered with disgusting floating things. It smelled slightly fishy, the way you'd expect a freshwater river to smell, but otherwise I wasn't overly concerned about catching some kind of illness or what have you from it.

(I have to admit, when I got home I ran a Google search and found out that the river, and the watershed of which it was a part, tested quite low for E coli or other revolting pollutants. Very reassuring, after the fact.)

I followed Rosemary down a gulley to the shoreline. We walked upstream along a footpath, the river flowing away from us on the left at quite a clip. I could see that the strength of the current would have given Iona Bazuski additional cause to forbid Renata from coming down here.

The shoreline was mostly stony, with only a thin stretch of sand disappearing into the water, so I gathered that swimming or wading wouldn't be much good unless you wore sneakers or sandals to protect your feet. Good for rock skipping, though, or testing your arm to see how far you could throw a stone. I resisted the impulse, although I did spot a very nice pebble that I picked up and put in my pocket. Rose quartz, if I wasn't mistaken.

"I don't see any old guy," Rosemary threw over her shoulder.

"Maybe he just comes down once in a while to fish."

She didn't answer.

"Are there fish in this river?"

"No idea."

We kept on, stepping over segments of tree branches that had washed ashore and were in the process of morphing into driftwood. At one point we passed the remains of a dead fish, some animal's leftover meal, apparently. The smell of which probably contributed to the overall aroma of the place.

"Hell's that?" Rosemary said, stopping.

I looked over her shoulder. We were approaching a bridge, which I gathered was the one where Stewart Street passed over the river. But it was the collection of debris under the bridge that had caught Rosemary's attention. Someone had used chunks of two-by-four, wooden pallets, unfolded cardboard boxes, garbage bags, and other junk to construct what appeared to be a shelter.

"What the hell you doing here?"

I nearly jumped out of my skin. Rosemary swivelled, fists up.

"Whoa, whoa, whoa." The man raised his arms defensively, a wild apparition with an uncombed beard and long grey hair. He wore a black-and-orange Hawaiian shirt, blue jeans, and rubber boots.

"You scared the fucking shit out of me!" Rosemary

exclaimed.

"What are you doing down here anyway?" He took a step backward, half-stumbling over a rock.

"Looking for you," I said. "Seems like we found you."

"Me? What the hell you want with me?"

"We want to talk to you." I took a step toward him, hands out, palms down. "We've got some questions to ask you."

"Questions? What about? I don't know a damned thing about nothing."

I gestured toward the junk under the bridge. "That yours?"

"Damned right it is, and I'm not moving out no matter what the overlords say. Is that who you're with? The damned township?"

"No." I put my foot up on a fallen log. "We're looking for a young man."

"What young man?"

"His name's Nathan Notwell. He comes down here from time to time, to walk along the shore and throw stones in the water."

"A lot of kids come down here. Sometimes I have to chase them off or they'll wreck my place. Little bastards. Young man? The name doesn't mean anything to me."

"Sometimes he's with a young woman and her dog. A little Yorkshire terrier named Butterscotch."

Light dawned in his watery blue eyes. "Oh, yeah, sure. Them two. They show up every now and again. I like that little dog. Comes right up and lets me rub her head."

"Nathan ever cause you any trouble?"

"Him? No. I'm usually fishing or picking crayfish for supper. He's polite enough. Wants to know what I'm doing, so we talk a bit. I don't mind."

"What's your name?"

"I'm Tom. Tom O'Toole."

I held out my hand. "I'm Mark Heron."

He pulled away. "I don't shake hands. Scared of damned germs. No offence, Mr. Heron."

"None taken. Tell me something."

"If I can."

"When was the last time you saw Nathan Notwell?"

He shook his head, his beard waggling back and forth. "I can't tell you that. I'm sorry. I don't even know what year it is, let alone day or month. After a while, you lose track."

Out of the corner of my eye, I saw that Rosemary had drifted over to the shelter and was looking inside. O'Toole noticed at the same time and bustled after her, pausing to pick up a hockey stick lying with other junk along the side of the bridge.

"Hey, hey now! Get out of there, dammit!"

Rosemary backed out. O'Toole brandished the hockey stick. Rosemary glared at him, bracing herself for a fight.

"There's no need!" I ran over, arms raised. "Put the stick down, Mr. O'Toole! We're leaving now."

"Get the hell out of here. You got no business sticking your nose into my property."

"You're on public property, you goddamned fool!" Rosemary retorted. "Don't you threaten me or I'll ram that thing so far up your ass you'll be spitting teeth."

I got between them, facing O'Toole. "We're leaving. No offence, remember? We're going now."

"Get the hell out of here and leave me alone."

I turned to face Rosemary. "Let's go. Now."

She gave me a searing look and walked away.

Back in the Escalade, she was still fuming. "Goddamn

son of a bitch, threaten me with a hockey stick. For two cents I'd go back down there and pound the shit out of him."

"What did you see?"

"What? What the hell are you talking about?"

"Settle down, Rosemary. It's done. What did you see inside his shelter?"

"Fuck. Shit. Piss."

I waited.

"Bunch of junk. He must be a dumpster diver. A wheel off a bicycle; a box of doorknobs, like he's got a door to use them on; a garbage bag full of clothes; skates; shit like that."

"Anything at all that might be connected to Nathan?"

She shook her head. "I only had a quick look. A lot of other stuff in there. Barely room for his bedroll."

"I'm concerned about his erratic behaviour."

"Are you kidding me? He's a fucking wackadoodle. The cops need to take a close look at him. Kids coming down here and then Nathan disappearing. Stinks like hell to me."

"You might be right. Or he might just be some homeless guy with mental health issues."

"Or he might be a psychopath, Mark. Come on. Get with it."

I hesitated a moment before giving in. "All right. Let's go report it."

CHAPTER

Eleven

Once again Rosemary took the lead, because she'd already been to the detachment office twice to talk to the detectives about Nathan. By the time we pulled into the parking lot and got out of the Escalade, she'd calmed down quite a bit, the adrenaline having been metabolized enough that her anger spike had modulated into grim determination to roast Tom O'Toole's butt on a spear.

She asked for Detective Constable Shepard, the person she'd talked to before, but he was off duty. She explained what she wanted, and someone came down from an upstairs office and let us in through the security door.

"We can talk in here," he said, leading us into a room with a table and several chairs. He closed the door behind me. "Sit down and tell me what this is about."

"I wanted to talk to the detective. Shepard. The one who's handling the disappearance of Nathan Notwell." Rosemary pulled out a chair and sat down. "I want to know if you guys have looked into the old geezer down at the river."

He opened a notebook and clicked a ballpoint pen.

"Can I have your names."

Rosemary gritted her teeth and supplied her name, address, and phone number. When it was my turn, I finished with a question. "What's your name?"

"Detective Constable Barnes. Now, how about one of you walk me through this."

I nodded at Rosemary and she gave him the basics of Nathan's disappearance. Barnes took a few notes, his eyes following the tip of his pen across the page. Rosemary mentioned Nathan's friend Renata and her story of having gone down to the river a few times with Nathan."

"So then you barged down there and rousted the old guy, is that right?" Barnes squinted up at her.

"He told me his name's Tom O'Toole," I said.

He wrote it down without looking at me. "Did he say he'd done anything to this Notwell?"

"No," Rosemary said, "of course not, but I think he's capable of it. He said he's threatened kids who come down there looking at his stuff. I think he's a wack job."

"His stuff. Like drugs and that sort of thing?"

She hesitated. "I didn't see anything like that."

"You looked at his stuff, too?"

"I looked inside, yeah. Mostly junk. Shit he must have picked out of dumpsters."

"No sign of drugs, or paraphernalia, anything like that."

"No, but this isn't about drugs; it's about a missing man."

Barnes said nothing, scratching a few more notes. Then he abruptly stood up and opened the door. "All right, thanks. I'll pass this along to Detective Constable Shepard, and if he needs to talk to you, he'll be in touch."

"That's it?" Rosemary glared at him. "You're not going

to follow up? Bring this guy in? Question him about what he did to Nathan? For chrissakes, the guy threatened to brain me with a hockey stick."

Barnes gestured to the open door. "We'll look into it, and if we need anything else from you, we'll be in touch. Thanks for coming in."

Out in the car, she did an admirable job of controlling herself this time. I let her fume in silence for a few moments as she wrestled with her anger, thinking that I now had a better understanding of her frustration with the way the authorities were handling Nathan's disappearance.

I would have thought that a missing person would be a hot-button case, an urgent priority where all the stops were pulled out and every available resource directed toward finding the man. Evidently, though, after two months without progress the investigation had cooled down and was now a back-burner item only.

It didn't seem right. But as far as I could tell, there wasn't anything we could do about it.

Rosemary grabbed her seatbelt and buckled up. "Let's go back there and do it ourselves. Break a bone or two and get him to admit what he's done."

"We're not sure he's done anything, Rosemary. And there's no point in using violence to coerce a statement that may end up not to be true after all."

"Only one way to find out."

I thought for a moment, and then said. "I've got a better idea. Let's go talk to a friend of mine."

CHAPTER
Twelve

The offices of the *Sentinel* weekly newspaper were located on the second floor of a building downtown on Gore Street, above a bookstore and a shop that sold wool, patterns, and knitting supplies. A freebie that usually ran to about sixteen pages, the paper covered local stories and featured regular columns about birds (which I read faithfully, as I've already mentioned), gardening (which I skimmed occasionally), and town politics (which I generally ignored).

The publisher and editor, Patrick Dillon, was an early-thirties journalism graduate from Oakville with a knack for making money. Five years ago, he bought the *Sentinel* out of receivership and moved to Perth to fulfill his dream of becoming the next great Canadian newspaperman. He was a tall, skinny kid with John Lennon glasses and tawny hair that was long, uncombed, and wavy.

I first met Patrick two summers ago. I was sitting on a park bench on the edge of the farmer's market downtown, enjoying the crowd and sketching whatever caught my eye. As it happened, I'd gotten an idea for a Christmas-themed cartoon, which the editors would soon be asking me for, and I was finishing up a quick sketch of it when this kid with a camera, notepad, and bemused smile passed behind the bench and looked over my shoulder.

He stopped, and I heard a chuckle.

I'd drawn a guy in a Santa Claus suit pulling down his beard to drink from a flask while a little girl looked up at him, mouth open. The caption read, "Wouldn't that be better on the rocks?"

I wasn't much of a Christmas guy, and the editor I was thinking of for this one wasn't either. Street-corner Santas were a time-honoured trope in the business, and since I hadn't done one in quite a while, I thought I'd give it a shot.

The kid sat down beside me and introduced himself. I stuck out my hand, and when I told him my name, he looked shocked.

"Not the real Mark Heron?"

"Not a fake one, I assure you."

"*The* Mark Heron?"

"I guess so."

"I had no idea you lived around here."

"Something new I'm trying out. I think I'll stay."

"Wow. I publish the *Sentinel*. I guess your work would be way too expensive for my budget."

I shrugged, closing my sketchbook. "You might be surprised. What can you afford?"

He mentioned an amount that would have insulted a Manhattan cab driver as a tip, but I nodded. "Sounds good to me."

"I publish once a week. Would that fit into your schedule somehow?"

"Why not. What sort of stuff are you looking for?"

"Anything you send me, I'll buy."

"Simplifies things."

"Do I dare ask about illustrations or spot drawings? I know you've done that kind of work before, too. I remember reading that you were responsible for all the section vignettes in *Saturday Magazine*—"

"That kind of stuff I do on commission. Once in a blue moon."

"Okay. I'll run to the office and grab a contract blank, if you're going to be here for a little while longer."

"Is your word good?"

He frowned. "Sure. Of course it is."

"So's mine. Let's skip the contract. When's your deadline?"

He told me.

"I'll send you a couple tomorrow afternoon," I said. "Pick what you want. How's that?"

"I can't believe this. Talk about the apple falling out of the tree right into my lap."

"Serendipity's a wonderful thing, son."

I held out my hand, and we shook on it.

When I got home, I pulled his last two issues out of the recycling bin and looked them over to get a sense of what he was trying to do with the paper. The writing and editing seemed solid, and the ads were well placed and numerous enough to be paying his way. As I tossed them back into the blue bin, I couldn't help smiling.

Should be fun.

And it has been, truth be told.

Rosemary and I followed Patrick into an adjoining office with high ceilings and large, arched windows with half-circle, multi-pane sections at the top. The furniture and fittings were all vintage, made of walnut, oak, and brass—that is, what you could see of them. Books were piled everywhere, alongside stacks of newspapers, old magazines, manual typewriters on rolling metal tables, and other collectibles and oddities.

Patrick moved a stack of file folders from a visitor's chair and gestured to Rosemary, who settled down on its edge. He found a spot in the corner for the files and came back to shoo a sleeping calico cat from the other chair so that I could sit down.

"I hope you're not allergic to cat fur," he said to Rosemary, dropping into the chair behind his desk. "We have four of them around here somewhere."

"I've got six. They're all feral. Mean as snakes."

"Oh."

"Thanks for taking the time to see us," I put in quickly. "I know how busy you are."

"Sure, no problem." He adjusted his glasses, glancing at Rosemary. "Today's the day I pick which submissions are good enough to run. I've actually got two freelancers contributing this week besides Larry—two more than I had last week. Larry's my only staff reporter at the moment."

"We won't take a lot of your time. We wanted to talk to you about your coverage of the Nathan Notwell disappearance."

"Who?"

"Nathan Notwell. A guy who disappeared in town the first week of June."

"Shit." Patrick turned to his computer and started clicking the mouse. "That's the week I was in Oakville. My mother's oldest brother's funeral. Command appearance, or whatever you'd call it. Larry covered for me and got the issue out. Wait. Here's the story."

He frowned, speed reading it. "Not much here. Larry

must have just worked from the OPP press release and that was it."

"Great stuff," Rosemary muttered.

"Sorry. We've been really short-staffed the last while. Like the police and just about every business you can think of since the pandemic."

"Whatever."

Patrick looked at me. "And we didn't do a follow-up?"

"I don't know."

"No, you didn't," Rosemary said. "There's been zip from anybody. Nobody gives a shit about a brain-damaged guy living with a cousin who's a single mom with nothing going for her."

"Not true." Patrick turned back to his monitor. "I'll run a query on his name."

We waited.

"Nope. You're right. Zip."

"Apparently there was another disappearance," I said. "A woman, in the spring?"

"Yeah, yeah. That one I remember." He ran another query. "Yessir. Here we are. Lucy Banner. Fifty-four years old. Music teacher. Disappeared March 22. A widow. Reported missing by her sister-in-law, Allison. They never found her."

He took off his glasses and rubbed his eyes. "We did a follow-up on that one a month later. Larry covered it for us. According to the sister-in-law, Lucy liked to attend music concerts all over the world. She'd just pick up and go without advance warning. The police couldn't find any trace of her leaving the country or booking into hotels here in Canada."

He put his glasses back on and frowned. "Hold on a sec."

He pawed around through the papers and miscellaneous stuff on his desk before pulling out a town map. "What's Notwell's address again?"

Rosemary recited it through clenched teeth.

Patrick circled the spot on the map, then turned back to the computer. "Uh . . . yeah, here it is."

He hunted on the map for a moment and then drew another circle. "Crap. Two blocks from each other. Look at that."

He held the map up so that we could see it. He was right: Nathan Notwell and Lucy Banner had lived in the same neighbourhood, only two blocks apart.

Rosemary swore. "They're connected."

"You may be right," I said.

"Damned right I'm right."

Patrick was back at his computer, typing again. "Okay, wait." He stared at the screen. "Here's another one. Last October. This kid was out jogging and never came home."

"In town?"

"Yeah. Peter Forrest, seventeen. Father's a widower . . . uh, John Forrest, housepainter and roofer. He filed a missing persons report but nothing turned up. Apparently the police thought he might have voluntarily left home. I remember this one too, but why haven't I been connecting these stories before now?"

"I don't know . . . stupidity?"

Patrick gave Rosemary a wan smile. "Maybe. Although I haven't slept more than four hours a night for the past two years. That might have something to do with it, too."

"What about any others, Patrick?" I asked, trying to deflect his attention away from her belligerence.

"Let's see." He scrolled down the list of hits. "Banner, Forrest, Forrest, Clement. Hang on. Oh, dear."

He tapped his mouse and stared at the monitor. "Yeah. Crap. Emily Clement. Librarian. Thirty-six years old. Disappeared while visiting her mother, Christine Clement, who lives on Rideau Ferry Road. Last August. Almost a year ago. She was weeding the flowers along the stone wall between the highway and her mother's front lawn, then all of a sudden she wasn't there. A neighbour thought he heard a splash and a scream, so the OPP Marine Unit came out with divers and a search-and-rescue team. They went up and down the Rideau but never found her."

He moved the mouse around, clicking. "Let me check on something. This story was filed by one of our freelancers, Dorothy Kerr. Her notes should be here. Just a minute."

I watched his eyes zip over the text displayed on the screen. He scrolled down, scrolled again, and then nodded.

"I'm looking through the notes she sent in a week later. She went back to talk to the witness a second time after the story ran. A retired guy named Darryl Morris. Lives on the other side of the road." Patrick chuckled. "'Stupid old fool,' Dorothy's got here. Apparently the guy fudged on the splash-and-scream bit afterwards. Crabbed about how noisy the highway gets. Some van with a bad muffler got his attention in particular."

"You mean when Kerr was interviewing him?" I asked.

"No, the day the woman disappeared."

"Four," Rosemary said.

"I believe," Patrick frowned at the screen, "the police are treating hers as an accidental drowning. Body never recovered."

"Bullshit. She was taken by the same sonofabitch who took Nathan and the others."

"There's absolutely no evidence to support that,

Rosemary."

"There's my gut evidence. They're connected, I'm telling you."

No one said anything for several long moments.

"You might be right," Patrick finally murmured. "We might just have a serial predator on our hands."

CHAPTER

Thirteen

I spent the afternoon dressed in grubby jeans and a plain orange T-shirt, pulling weeds in my herb garden. Green therapy, I suppose you could call it.

This side of the house faced west, overlooking acres of hay, as I may have mentioned before, and was dominated from front to back by the solarium. At the roadside corner, visible from the driveway, was an elbow-shaped garden in which red poppies grew in front of tall hollyhocks, mostly dark purple and pink. At the backfield corner, in another wraparound plot, were irises. The fragrant kind. One of the sweetest smelling creations ever to grace this planet.

In between, fronting the solarium and facing the western sun, were my herbs. Sage, lemon balm, lavender, mint, thyme, and an enormous chives plant sitting like a big green spider in the middle.

Along the back of the studio, another garden was devoted to sweet bergamot, a.k.a. bee balm, but it pretty much looked after itself, so I spent my time with the herbs, pulling weeds and thinning a bit to make sure the lavender and sage had room to expand, should they so desire.

In the fall I dried a lot of the fragrant herbs and chopped them up for winter potpourris as a way to remind myself what I had to look forward to when the snow finally disappeared the following spring. Otherwise, I used them fresh in my cooking in the summer or dried in the winter as a remembrance of things past, or I just rubbed the odd leaf between my thumb and fingers to enjoy the heavenly odour.

On this particular day, the work helped lower my stress level after a rough morning, and so you can imagine how disappointed I was when the phone rang, just as I was taking a little breather on my folding stool.

I'd brought the portable phone outside, in case the doctor's office needed to reach me or an acquiring editor wanted to discuss another paperback collection of my work. I didn't have my reading glasses handy to see the call display, so I just went ahead and answered it.

"Mark! How the hell are you?"

"Bob, long time no hear. Doing fine. How about you?"

"Good, good. May's looking forward to her Paris shopping trip."

I took off my hat and wiped my brow with my forearm. "That's right, I forgot you were going. When do you head out?"

"Day after tomorrow. Actually, that's why I'm calling."

I reached for my water bottle and took a swig. "Oh?"

"Since you issued the big decree of no party, no fuss, no nothing, we've decided to stop in tomorrow and wish you an early happy birthday. We'll just stay overnight and catch an early flight the next morning out of YOW for Brussels. How's that sound?"

"Sounds great."

Bob Champion was an old friend. He'd recently retired

as publisher of *Saturday Magazine*, which I've mentioned several times as a good customer of mine, and I was under the impression he was determined to enjoy his new-found freedom with a vengeance. The last time we spoke, a few weeks ago, he'd mentioned that he'd booked the Grand Tour, as he called it, a three-month vacation in Europe, but I'd lost track of when it was supposed to happen.

"No need to make a fuss," he said. "We're simple folks, as you know. May's a vegetarian, but she eats dairy, and I'll eat whatever you put in front of me. Although to me you'll always be the king of the grill. Not to jiggle your elbow or anything."

"No, no. That'll be fine. What time shall I expect you?"

"Flight leaves at eleven in the morning. We'll rent a car and drive down from Ottawa, so, say one or one thirty?"

"I'll have some lunch ready for you when you get here."

"That'll be wonderful." He paused. "So, how are you really doing?"

"I'm fine, actually. Not bad at all."

"Not all traumatized by the big Seven-Oh?"

I forced a laugh. "No, not really."

"Well, you remember how bent out of shape I was when I hit sixty. It wouldn't surprise me a bit if you were lying awake at three in the morning going over your lifetime of sins."

"My heart is pure, Bob, and I sleep like a baby."

"Sure you do. May sends her love. See you tomorrow."

CHAPTER

Fourteen

The following morning, after browsing through my cook books, I took a look in my refrigerator and didn't see everything I wanted. I made another list and drove into town, where I picked up some nice steak, a bag of potatoes (which I'd forgotten to buy on Friday), two loaves of Texas toast, tzatziki dip, and an assortment of fresh vegetables suitable for grilling, including a couple of eggplants.

I stopped in the liquor store before leaving town and bought a few bottles of wine, white and red, and a quart of Bob's favourite rye. By the time I got home it was just past eleven thirty. Bob and May would be in the air right now, so I washed up the vegetables and got to work. The first thing I did was fry a pound of bacon. As it was cooking, I sliced some gruyere and cheddar cheese, buttered both sides of half the loaf of Texas bread, and set everything aside for later.

Bob was a fiend for grilled cheese sandwiches, and so was I. That took care of our lunch, but what about May?

Easy enough. I made a Greek orzo dish, rough cut a fresh head of lettuce, sliced some cherry tomatoes, a green pepper, and some mushrooms, tossed it with chopped oregano from the garden, and after a moment's thought, fried one of the slices of toast and cubed it for croutons. There were several kinds of salad dressing in the fridge I could offer her, so I covered everything with plastic wrap and refrigerated it until serving time.

I also made a fresh fruit salad, which I would serve with the tzatziki dip on the side.

I cleaned up and mixed a marinade for the steak, bagged each piece and poured it in, then popped them into the fridge as well. It was a preparation Bob particularly liked, and I knew he would be looking forward to it. I put the potatoes into a bowl, drizzled in some olive oil, sprinkled a generous amount of rosemary and thyme, and covered them to roast with peeled carrots on the grill for dinner.

All straight from memory, according to the Bob Champion guide to fine eating. With a couple of vegetarian Hail Marys for May added in.

They arrived in their rental Audi shortly before one. Bob climbed out of the passenger seat, dapper in his white chinos and blue shirt, a tan jacket draped over his arm. His hair was whiter than when I'd last seen him—completely white, now—but his familiar Sam Elliott moustache was still shot through with dark brown.

We shook hands and embraced, his widow's peak brushing the top of my forehead.

"Christ, it's good to see you, kid." He held me at arm's length. "You look great! Really great!"

"So do you. Looks like you already got a start on your continental tan."

He laughed. "Time at the cottage. I didn't want to go over there looking like some pasty-faced office clerk. This is May."

We'd never met before, although we'd spoken to each other briefly on the phone when I'd call Bob for a chat. She was his third wife. I'd liked the first one, despised the second, and now here I was once again, face to face with a new Champion spouse.

She slung a small brown handbag over her shoulder and held out her hand. "Hello, Mark. It's nice to finally meet in person."

She was tall and slender, her Asian features delicate and refined, and her voice was a soft contralto which, although I'd heard it before electronically, was hypnotizing in person. She wore a tan linen suit consisting of an open-front jacket over a white T-shirt, and trousers with a slight flair at the cuffs. Her raven hair was long and draped over her shoulders, and her shoes, amusingly, were brown Reeboks that matched her bag.

"If you want to give me your keys," I said, "I'll grab your luggage."

"Relax, old guy. I've already got it." Bob had slipped around to the back of the Audi. May used the key fob to pop the trunk, and he pulled out two black carry-on bags, the kind with wheels and telescopic handles.

"Okay, then. Please step this way." I led them inside.

"Oh, this is lovely," May said.

Bob hefted the bags. "Where shall I put these?"

"If you want to leave them there," I said, "I'll have the houseboy take them up to your room."

"Funny."

"Top of the stairs, first door on the right."

As he clopped upstairs, I smiled at May and pointed to a doorway on the left. "Dining room, and through that to the kitchen."

She peeked in and murmured something polite.

"Hallway straight ahead. Door at the end is the kitchen; door on the right is my studio, door on the left is the powder room."

"That's my cue."

As the powder room door closed, Bob came back downstairs. I took him into the living room.

"Nice," he said. "Where'd you get all the antiques?"

"Auctions, mostly." I led him through the room, which I'd decorated with a Shaker secretary desk, a glass-front bookcase, a sofa, a couple of wingback chairs, and other items of furniture. The artwork on the walls was Canadian, paintings and watercolours by artists such as Toni Onley and, happily, a piece by Frederick Simpson Coburn, my favourite. It was a beautiful winter landscape with a horse-drawn wagon in the foreground, rolling brown-and-white hills behind, and a big, grey, cloudy morning sky overhead. Oil and canvas, 1922, 65 centimeters by 79 centimeters, entitled *A Winter Morning in Quebec*. There was another one much like it in the National Gallery. This painting was one of my favourite possessions.

He circulated around, examining everything with a critical eye, and stopped at a Remington bronze.

"Reproduction," I said.

He grinned. "Who cares, right? It's gorgeous."

I opened a set of louvered doors. "The solarium."

He strolled in. "I saw it from outside. Nice touch."

I'd settled on a more casual look with the decorating in here—wicker, glass-top tables, and lots of plants.

May came in behind us. "Wow, this is very nice, Mark. You have a beautiful home." She had changed into a pair of plaid shorts and a beige sleeveless T-shirt.

"I can show you the studio later, if you'd rather have some lunch now."

Bob looked at May, who said, "I've been looking forward to seeing where you work."

"This way, then."

I took them through the door at the far end of the solarium into a small mudroom. Egress to the great beyond on the right; ingress to the studio on the left.

Although a decent amount of natural light filled the room, I flicked on the fluorescents. Bob barged ahead, making a beeline for the worktable where I'd left my Halloween roughs to marinate in their own juices for a day or two. He put on his reading glasses, picked up one, and frowned at it.

A man in a ridiculous rabbit suit slumps in a chair beside the front door where a treat basket has been pillaged. He looks decidedly queasy. His wife, hands on her hips, says, "I should have told you the ones wrapped in pink paper are for the neighbour's dog."

Bob put it back down on the table. "Hmmm." He moved to the next, in which two cats sit on a rug, one of them having just thrown up a Halloween treat. The second cat says, "I keep trying to tell them mint's toxic, but do they listen to anything I say?"

He grunted, picking up the third, which was the one with the two kids with healthy food in their goody bags. The corner of his mouth twitched.

Bob never laughed at my work—or anyone else's, for that matter. He'd always maintained a poker face when considering submissions, especially in person, and it was almost impossible to know what he liked or disliked.

Almost.

The mouth twitch was his tell. That was the famous Robert Champion, publisher to the gods, repressing a chuckle.

CHAPTER

Fifteen

Lunch was a success. Bob sent me back to the grill for another round of sandwiches which, as always, he consumed with gusto. May expressed pleasure at her Greek orzo dish, and chose an oregano dressing for her salad.

After eating and a quick trip to the washroom, Bob took a cup of coffee into the solarium and pulled out his phone. The new guy, apparently, needed advice and guidance from the departing genius, and it might take a while. May helped me clean up, after which I suggested a walk, so she could see the rest of the property.

I kept a pair of walking shoes in the mudroom, so I sat down on a bench to put them on. I looked at her Reeboks and said, "Will those be all right?"

"They take me everywhere."

"It's a cleared path the entire way," I said, "so they should be fine."

I grabbed a couple of water bottles from the mini-fridge and opened the door for her. We started out along the eastern perimeter, which curved south toward the back of the property. There was another lot between mine and the intersection of Tennyson Road and Muldoon Side Road. About ten acres in size, it ran down Muldoon Side Road, past the abandoned house I could see at the rear of my place. The lot was unused and overgrown with weeds and trees. Since a few of the trees were oak, and I could fill a basket with acorns when I walked the path in the autumn, I didn't mind the fact that it had kept its natural characteristics.

"You and Bob have been friends for a long time," May said, hands clasped behind her back as we strolled along.

"Yes, we have. We were neighbours when he was in school."

"Oh?"

"I was living in an apartment downtown and teaching part-time at OCAD." I'd been an instructor at the Ontario College of Art and Design two years after graduation, an alumnus lucky enough to score a job with my alma mater.

"Bob moved in across the hall. He was in third year at Ryerson, doing his journalism degree. We met in the hallway and he recognized me from a piece that had appeared in a local weekly. One of my strips had just been syndicated and they gave me a nice bit of coverage. Anyway, he wouldn't leave me alone after that."

She laughed. "He wouldn't?"

"Kept slipping pieces of paper under my door. A couple of sentences describing a gag cartoon. No drawings, just text. 'A bride and groom stand at the altar. The groom says, "I think I forgot to tie the tin cans to the back of the car."' Bob would write on top of each one, 'Is this funny?' They were terrible. I'd write back, 'No,' and put it under his door."

"Oh dear."

"Finally when I saw him in the hallway again, I asked him what the hell was going on. 'Are you trying to become a cartoonist? Because if you are, you'd better find something better to do with your free time.'"

"Was he crushed?"

I smiled. "Not in the slightest. He said, 'You're helping to teach me the art of humour. What's funny and what's not. That way, when I'm considering cartoon submissions for my magazine, I can make an educated decision.'"

"I said, 'What the hell magazine is that?' and he said, 'The one I'm going to publish as soon as I graduate.'"

She laughed. "Sounds just like him."

"After that, I got him to knock and bring them in so we could talk about them over a beer. It was the start of a very long friendship."

We'd reached the fallen tree at the back, so I gave her a bottle of water and sat down. "What about you, May? How'd you get into modelling?"

She sipped water and watched a robin land on a tree branch nearby. "It was my mom's fault."

"Oh?"

She laughed. "My mother's a public person as well. I was an awkward, introverted fourteen-year-old and she decided to do something about it."

"What does she do? Your mom?"

"She's a concert pianist. Wen Zhang? She specializes in the Romantics. Schumann, Liszt, Mendelssohn, Schubert."

"Good lord. I've heard of her."

She smiled. "I'm sure you have. Anyway, she enrolled me in a modelling class to teach me good posture, how to walk, and how to develop self-confidence."

"Obviously, it worked."

"Thank you. Are you sure you want to hear this? It's very boring."

"Are you kidding? Please, keep going."

She sat down next to me. "My mother entered me in a Victoria's Secret modelling contest when I was sixteen. There were a lot of other girls, but I won. It was kind of incredible. I felt like an impostor, an amateur against all the others, but I guess I didn't realize how much I'd learned at modelling school. Anyway, I signed with an agency and walked the runway for Victoria's Secret for the next couple of years. Then it was Michael Kors, Tom Ford, and Ralph Lauren."

"Holy cow."

"It was fun. I loved it. The excitement, the clothes, the crowds. There's nothing else in the world like it. It's like walking a ledge fifty storeys up. Don't look down, and don't look behind you."

"And you were what, sixteen?"

"Yeah. When I turned twenty-one, I signed a new contract. My own, without my mother's signature on it. With a different agency. I was already being told I was too old for the runway, so this new agency moved me over to studio work. I started getting into magazines, and before long I became the go-to Asian face for Ralph Lauren."

"Wait, you were too old for the runway at twenty-one?"

She laughed. "The average age of a runway model is anywhere between fourteen and twenty-five, but twenty is usually the cut-off date for most of the high-end designers. After that, you're pretty much done and they're looking in a different direction for someone else."

"You *do* realize," I said, "that I'm about to turn seventy. And you're talking about twenty-one being too old."

She shrugged, smiling. "It's all relative, isn't it? Ageism is everywhere, right across the board. In broadcasting, in publishing, and—oh yes!—in the fashion industry."

"Amazing. Please, go on."

"There's not much else to tell." She took another sip of water. "Thanks to the new agency, I started getting covers. *Cosmo, Vogue, Harper's Bazaar.* A whole new level of wow. And a makeup thing with Estée Lauder. They were starting to talk about me as one of the top Asian models in the world."

My mouth must have been hanging open a bit, because she waved the water bottle at me. "You've never heard of me, have you?"

"Um, actually, no." My face grew warm. "Sorry. I don't submit to those magazines, so I never look at them."

She smiled. "That's quite all right. It's a relief to have a friend I can start from scratch with. Just be myself."

"Well, I have to admit I've never been interested in fashion. I don't think I've ever even spoofed it."

"Don't worry about it. Please!"

"So how'd you meet Bob?"

She looked away, watching a red squirrel mooch around on the path behind us. "I was twenty-eight. *Saturday Magazine* was profiling me as a successful Canadian looking for new horizons. I met him on the set a couple of times, and we chatted. He asked me out to dinner. I'd liked the kind of questions he asked, even though he wasn't writing the article, so I said yes to dinner. We went out. He was the consummate gentleman. We began to date regularly. He asked my advice on things to do with the magazine and took my answers seriously. Even implemented some of my suggestions. He kind of swept me off my feet, I guess. When he started talking about marriage, I was excited."

"He's very lucky to have you," I said.

"You should talk to my mother about that."

"So are you all the way retired now?"

She shook her head. "I still work part time. While we're in Europe I've got a shoot scheduled in Milan for *Vogue Italia*. They're doing a feature on 'sophisticated older women.' I'm flattered! Anyway, I get the cover, so it's all good."

Piano music began to leak from her handbag. Schumann? Her mom? She pulled out her cellphone and looked at the call display before answering it.

"Yes, Bob." She listened. "Just a sec."

She handed me the phone. "He wants a word with you."

Puzzled, I accepted the phone. "Yep?"

"Some biker girl just drove in and wants to talk to you. She's pretty insistent on it. Who the hell is she, anyway?"

I chuckled. "Her name's Rosemary. Offer her a Coke and tell her I'll be there in a few minutes."

CHAPTER

Sixteen

"We have to talk," Rosemary said.

We were sitting on the patio in the back yard, looking across the lawn at the treeline, about a hundred meters away. Heat absorbed by the ground from the afternoon sun rose again in shimmering waves.

Bob had turned off his cellphone for the occasion, sipping his first rye and ginger of the afternoon, and May sat next to Rosemary with a cup of tea.

"Talk about what?" I lit a cigar. It was a signal to Rosemary that she could smoke if she wished, that Bob and May wouldn't mind, but she might have been too agitated to pick up on it.

"Alone." She glanced at Bob suspiciously.

"The cousin of Rosemary's friend has disappeared," I said to Bob and May. "He's twenty-seven but intellectually challenged. Rosemary's trying to find out what happened to him, and I'm trying to help."

Bob frowned. "How can *you* help?"

"You say that as though I'm a useless old geezer."

"Pfthht. You know what I mean. That sort of thing falls

under the purview of the local police. Which is . . ."

"The OPP. They've done their thing, but they've hit a dead end. We're trying to see if there's something that's been missed."

"I found Emily Clement's mother," Rosemary said to me. "We need to go talk to her."

"Oh?" Once again she'd managed to snag my interest with a well-baited hook.

"Bryan was nagging me this morning about going for a check up, whatever, and he said the receptionist was nice. I wouldn't mind talking to her. Turns out it's Emily's mom."

Smoke leaked from my mouth as a I listened.

"Is this a different missing person?" Bob wanted to know.

I nodded. "Looks like there might be four altogether. All from this area. All in the last year or so."

"Sounds like a story."

"The publisher of the local paper's working on it."

"Who's that?"

"Patrick Dillon."

"Don't know him." Bob sipped his drink and suddenly frowned. "Wait, wait, wait, wait. That wouldn't be Sean Dillon's son, would it?"

"Hunh. Yep."

"For crying out loud! Is this where he ended up? What is it, some rag-tag weekly that's almost all ads and little stories covering the Legion turkey dinner and the local quilting club?"

"Ballpark, yeah, but you're selling him short. He's very good, and he's really making a go of it."

"Well, he certainly has the smarts. He could have parachuted into any of the major dailies and become a star within six months."

"Oh, he'll be a star. In his own time, and in his own way." I peered at Bob through a veil of smoke. "He reminds me a lot of you at that age. Full of piss and vinegar."

"So can we go now?" Rosemary demanded.

I looked at her. "What day is today?"

"Sunday. Why, did you forget? Having an Alzheimer's moment?"

"Is the doctor's office open today?"

"No, I . . ."

"We could probably wait until tomorrow."

"Can't we find out where she lives? Talk to her there?"

I moved my hand in a calming gesture. "I have guests, Rosemary. We can't just charge off and leave them sitting here. It would be very rude."

She muttered something that was decidedly rude.

"I'll pick you up in the morning," I assured her.

"Mark," Bob said, "can I talk to you alone for a minute?"

Rosemary muttered something else, but I rolled my eyes. It was an old joke between Bob and myself. A parody of the sitcom cliché where an aside between the main character and his best friend is called for in the script. We had no intention of getting up and moving off by ourselves, stage right, being far too comfortable and far too lazy.

"Sure, Bob. What is it?"

"This sounds a little sketchy, don't you think? Involving yourself in these cases the police are already handling? Do they think they're connected?"

"They don't have the first frigging clue," Rosemary said.

I drew on my cigar and forced the smoke out between narrowed lips. "Patrick's started looking at them with us, and I think he agrees that they may be the doings of a single person."

"If there's someone out there, a serial predator of some kind, then it sounds a little dangerous for a seventy-year-old to be gallivanting around sticking his nose where it doesn't belong."

"I appreciate your concern. Really, I do. But I must remind you, rather firmly, that I'm not seventy yet."

May turned to Rosemary. "Is it dangerous? For you and Mark?"

Rosemary frowned, and I could read her mind as she prepared to say, "Why would you give a shit, lady?" But she didn't say it. Instead, she shrugged.

"We'll take every precaution," I told May. "And I think we'll push Patrick out in front of us and follow safely behind."

"If he smells a big story," Bob said, "something that'll put his paper on the map, he'll be like a dog after a bone. I know I would."

"Q.E.D.," I said, smiling at him. He'd just demonstrated the accuracy of my comparison of Patrick to him at a younger age.

Bob looked at his watch and gave a start. "Crap. Would you folks excuse me? I was expecting a call five minutes ago."

"Sure. Can I freshen your drink for you?"

"I can do it myself, thanks, Mark."

May turned to Rosemary. "Do you live in town?"

I examined the ash on the tip of my cigar.

"No. South of town."

"Are you working?"

"Yeah. Grocery store."

I picked up the tea pot and May nodded. As I refilled

her cup, I glanced at Rosemary but she was having none of it. I could take my conciliatory gestures and shove them up my wusket.

"My sister works in a grocery store downtown," May said. "Toronto. Right in Chinatown."

"Is that right."

"People can be so rude to her, it's upsetting. The elders are fine, of course, but some of the younger ones have no sense of propriety. They say the first thing that comes into their heads, and it's almost always negative."

"Yeah." Rosemary took out her cigarettes and lit one. I took it as a positive sign. Finally.

"I suppose you get a lot of that, too," May said.

"You're not kidding."

"This young man that disappeared. What's his name?"

"Nathan."

"And his cousin's your friend."

Rosemary exhaled a stream of smoke. "Yeah. We worked in the egg factory together." She pulled over my ashtray and tapped in it. "I was seventeen. She's twelve years older than me. She kind of showed me the ropes. I lasted almost a year, but I couldn't stand the smell. I got out, but Grace is still there. She and I are still friends."

"Did you have a chance to finish high school?"

Rosemary narrowed her eyes. "No."

"I didn't either. I started working when I was sixteen and never had a chance to go back. I'd like to get my equivalency, at least. Then I could say I have at least a Grade Twelve education. Maybe in a year or two."

Rosemary looked at her from the corner of her eye. I could tell she wasn't sure whether or not she should believe May.

"May's a model," I said.

"Yeah, I know." She looked directly at May for the first time. "I've seen you on the magazines in the stores. You always look so beautiful."

"Thank you, Rosemary."

"You're even more incredible in person."

May set aside her tea cup. "You know something I've never done before?"

"What's that?"

"Ride on a motorcycle. What say you take me up and down the road a bit? I'm dying to know what it's like."

"Are you sure?" Rosemary looked from her to me.

"Do I need a helmet?" May asked.

"Yeah, but I've got an extra one. I've got it clipped to the back seat in case I have to rush the old guy to the hospital or something." She gave me a look.

May stood up. "Then what are we waiting for?"

CHAPTER

Seventeen

It was an early start to a Monday as Bob and May were up at three thirty in the morning in order to leave at four to make their six o'clock flight to Frankfurt.

I got up with them and made breakfast, carried May's bag to the car for her, and watched as their tail lights disappeared between the blue spruces as the Audi accelerated away in the direction of Ottawa.

I went back inside and cleaned up the kitchen, ran the vacuum around the house a bit, stripped the bedding from the guest room and put it in the wash, emptied the ash trays, and generally tidied up. There was no point in going back to bed. I knew from long experience that once I was up, I was up for the day.

My reward for the busy work was to find a place for my birthday gift.

Bob and May had presented me with a framed and signed original drawing of a single-panel gag cartoon by the late great Leo Cullum, one of my favourites of all time. Three guys are sitting at a bar, and the middle one is holding his beer glass to his ear. The caption reads: "Hey

. . . I can hear the brewery."

For years I'd kept this one under the plastic of my desk blotter, along with several others clipped out of magazines over the years. I found it in *Penthouse*, which, along with *Playboy*, was at the time an excellent market for us, because they took our work as seriously as their, uh, other material. Well, almost.

I met Leo once at a convention in San Francisco, not long after I'd received the Governor General's Award. He had no idea what that was, but he congratulated me on it just the same. A former Marine pilot who fought in the Vietnam War, he spent the rest of his career flying for commercial carriers while cartooning on the side. He sold more than eight hundred to *The New Yorker* alone, and was one of their most popular cartoonists.

I've always been a fan.

It took very little thought to decide on a spot in the studio where I would hang it up. In a corner safe from destructive sunlight was a framed photograph that had been taken fifteen years ago at the aforementioned convention. In the picture I sat at a table with Leo, Mort Drucker, Sam Gross, Gahan Wilson, Jack Davis, and Al Jaffee. It had started out as a *Mad* magazine gathering of the clan, but we single-panel guys had quickly infiltrated it in order to rub elbows with royalty. George Booth, passing by on his way to cartoon greatness, had stopped and taken the photo, using Al's camera.

Whenever I looked at it now, I felt a mixture of pride and despair. I'd been a part of that group, accepted and welcomed by some of the greatest of them all. How could I not feel proud? At the same time, the photo reminded me that I was the only one who was still alive. Leo passed away in 2010; Jack, in 2016; Gahan, in 2019; Mort, in 2020;

George, in 2022; Sam and Al, in 2023.

Memento mori.

I hung Leo's cartoon on the wall next to the photo and stepped back to admire the two of them for a long moment.

"Rest in peace, brothers," I murmured.

I had to use the GPS to find Rosemary's place. I drove into town, continued out the other side, and came to Otty Lake Side Road earlier than I thought I would. I followed it for about half a kilometer before reaching a T-intersection, with Wild Life Road running off to the left. According to the signs, the township dump could be found down there somewhere. The location of which was something that had never occurred to me to wonder about before.

Across the intersection was a garage. Harley-Davidson signs festooned the place, including on top of a big pole at the edge of the road, along with signs advertising motor oil, parts, and other incomprehensible motorcycle-related things. Above the door leading into the office another sign said, "Nolan Repairs and Restoration."

I turned onto Wild Life Road, wondering how on earth it had gotten that name, and immediately came to a driveway on my left. There were two mailboxes: one for "B. Nolan" and the other for "Nolan Repair." None for Rosemary, it would seem.

I turned in, and after a few meters came to a well-tended lawn and a white Airstream trailer on the left. Rosemary's Harley was parked in a small shelter built onto the end of the trailer. It was covered with a tarp to protect it from road dust and other miscellaneous assailants. Farther up the driveway I could see a frame bungalow with a pickup truck and an older model Toyota parked in front. The cousin's house, no doubt.

I rapped on the door and heard some mild cursing. After a moment I saw her peering out a little window beside the door. "I'll be there in a minute. Sit and wait. How do you take your damned coffee?"

"Cream, one sugar."

"No cream. Two percent." The face disappeared.

I looked around and spotted a picnic table set up nearby under a crab apple tree. I went back to the Escalade, grabbed a cigar from the travelling case in the centre console, and sat down at the picnic table.

She'd made a small garden along the front of the Airstream and planted it with petunias, marigolds, and pansies. The siding on the trailer was clean, and the vents on the top were in good shape. The lawn had recently been cut, and the steps leading up to the door looked safe to walk on.

It was a nice morning. The sky was clear, and a light breeze took the edge off the sun's heat. I lit the cigar, cupping the end in my hands until it was fired up, then I turned around and rested my back against the edge of the table.

A black cat wandered around from behind the trailer and froze when it saw me. It watched me for a few moments, then very slowly turned around and disappeared back the way it had come. I remembered Rosemary saying she had feral cats. That must have been one of them.

It was a pleasant spot. Rosemary had made a decent home for herself. An attempt to find a little peace of mind. She was such a tightly wound person; so intense. Perhaps if I were able to help her find out what had happened to Nathan Notwell, she'd let go of it and move on with her life.

But then, of course, we'd added another person, hadn't we? Emily Clement. Thought to have fallen into the Rideau River and drowned, her body swept away downstream, never to be found.

No peace of mind for us right now, I thought, watching cigar smoke wind up into the branches above my head. Not for Rosemary Nolan, and not for Mark Heron either. Caught up in this quixotic attempt to make sense of an insensible, unmindful universe.

The door opened and Rosemary came out with a mug in each hand and a cigarette in the corner of her mouth. She used her elbow to close the trailer door behind her. I swung my legs around and faced her as she sat down and put one of the mugs in front of me.

"It's too early." She reached down for a coffee can and put it up on the table. "The doctor's office is only just opened. Let's give her time to get settled in so she'll talk to us instead of being all hassled and shit."

"Sounds good to me." I tried the coffee. It was decent, although a little stronger from the milk than it would have been with cream.

"I went to see the cop. After I left your place. The detective."

"What did he have to say?"

"He's pretty much an asshole. 'Don't be interfering in an ongoing police investigation.' I said, 'So how can I be interfering in an ongoing investigation when you guys are sitting here with your thumb up your ass doing fuck all?'"

"You didn't actually say that, Rosemary."

"Damned right I did. He didn't like it too much."

"I can imagine."

"So I said, 'What are you doing about the fact that

there's four people that've been kidnapped by this psycho? That we know of?' And he just brushed it off. 'There's no evidence that anyone's been kidnapped,' he says. Well, fuck me. That's a lot of bullshit."

She was clearly wound up tightly this morning. To change the subject, I said, "I'm glad you had a chance to meet Bob and May yesterday."

"Yeah."

"You and May seemed to hit it off."

She drank coffee, tapped her cigarette, fidgeted, and looked around. "She's nice."

"Will you stay in touch with her?" I'd seen them exchange Instagram and Messenger co-ordinates, or whatever people do these days instead of e-mail and the telephone.

"I'll see. She'll probably be way too busy to bother."

"Somehow I don't think so. I think you made a friend."

She gave me a look. "My friends are like Grace. Not like May Wen."

I shrugged. "It's none of my business. I just think you shouldn't sell her short. She's a human being too, you know."

Rosemary dropped her cigarette into the coffee can and stood up. "Hell with it. Let's get moving."

CHAPTER

Eighteen

The Birch Street Medical Centre was an older, three-storey building with offices for dentists, general practitioners, and a psychiatrist. It also had a lab on one side of the main floor and a physiotherapist outfit on the other side.

Dr. Stevenson's office was on the second floor, to the right off the staircase and directly across the hallway. I led the way into the waiting room, which was surprisingly empty. The receptionist sat behind a sheet of plexiglass with a hole cut in it for patients to talk through. I wondered if perhaps it was there to protect her from people who might be prone to lunging over the counter if they didn't like her service.

She wore a headset and appeared to be talking to someone on the phone. I waited for her to finish her conversation, but before I could open my mouth she removed the headset and frowned.

"I'm sorry, Dr. Stevenson's not seeing anyone today. Did you have an appointment?"

"No, I—"

"He's at the hospital, and all appointments are cancelled. A water pipe burst in the building this morning and half the offices are flooded. If you want to call later—"

"Are you Christine Clement?"

She blinked at me. "Yes. Why? Are you with the cleaners?"

"Uh, no. We wanted to talk to you about something else. Looks like this is a bad time, though."

She sighed. Standing up, she came out into the waiting room and motioned for us to sit down. "What can I do for you?"

"Are you sure it's okay to interrupt your work?"

"That was the last of today's appointments I had to reschedule. I need a break. What's this about?"

I glanced at Rosemary to include her in what I was about to say. "My name's Mark Heron, and this is Rosemary. We're looking into the disappearance of a young man who went missing in June. His cousin is a friend of Rosemary's, and we understand your daughter disappeared last year. We're wondering if there might be a connection."

"I'm not sure I want to have this conversation."

"We completely understand. We just thought maybe you could tell us something about Emily's disappearance that might help us find Nathan."

Christine sat down. "I don't see how."

"It's a long shot, I admit." I glanced again at Rosemary, so she would know she could jump in at any time. "We understand the police believe that Emily fell in the river and drowned."

She nodded, eyes down.

"Someone said they heard a scream and a splash."

She shook her head in disgust. "That old drunk. He's just a damned old fool."

"A Mr. Darryl Morris. Lives across the road from you."

"He's full of crap. He never heard Emily at all. He was too busy sitting in his lawn chair getting plastered."

"Can you tell us what happened that day?"

"Sure." She chewed on her lower lip. "Why not? Emily always came to visit on Sundays because the library's closed and she has the day off. It was the middle of the afternoon. She went out for some fresh air and said she'd weed the little garden I keep along the stone wall out front. It's about three feet high. The wall, I mean. Someone made it out of field stones a hundred years ago or something. Anyway, I planted perennials in front of it so it would look nice from the road, and she wanted to pull the weeds. When she hadn't come back in for quite a while I went out and looked all around the yard and couldn't see her. I walked up and down the highway. It's busy, right before the bridge, and cars go too fast along there. I was afraid I'd find her body in the ditch, that she'd been hit, but there was nothing. Her car was still in the driveway, so she hadn't gone home without telling me. I called her cellphone anyway, and there was no answer. I waited a while longer, got really frightened, and called 911."

"Had you heard anything unusual outside? A loud noise of any kind?"

"No. The police asked me all these questions then. It's the same answer now. Yes, she liked to go down to the river and walk along the shore a ways, but she could swim real good. The bottom line is I didn't hear anything and I didn't see anything. She just vanished and never came back."

"Nathan was sitting in the park," Rosemary said, "just sitting there after work, and he never made it home. Only two blocks away from the house where he lived. There has to be a connection. There *has* to be."

Christine shook her head. "A year apart. Different places. I don't know, dear. I can't see it."

The outer door opened and a young man walked in. He wore grey coveralls and work boots. He stopped when he saw us.

"I'm sorry, Mrs. Clement. I didn't know you were still here. Most people went home."

She managed a smile for him. "That's all right, Martin. I was just rescheduling the doctor's appointments. I'll be leaving soon."

"Did you see any water coming down through the ceiling? It's mostly at the far end of the building."

"No, I didn't see anything, thankfully."

"I just have to check around. Is it okay?"

She waved a hand. "Of course."

He wandered into the inner office, eyes up.

"Sorry for the interruption," she said to us. "Anyway, I just don't think there's anything I can tell you that the police don't already know."

"What about her friends?" Rosemary persisted. "Maybe she said something to them about someone bothering her."

"She was very introverted," Christine replied. "She didn't have a lot of friends. The police talked to them and talked to her co-workers at the library, but nobody knew anything."

"We've probably taken up enough of your time," I said. It was apparent that we weren't going to get anything from her that would help us with Nathan.

The cleaning guy wandered back in. "Don't see anything. Looks like you'll be good to go as soon as they give the green light."

"Oh, that's great, Martin. Thank you."

"No problem."

His name was embroidered on a patch below his left collarbone, and the shoulder flashes identified the company he worked for as "Butler Brothers Janitorial Services." He was a small-framed twenty-something with a buzz cut and an acne-scarred complexion.

"Funny," I said, "I thought butlers just answered the door, and somebody else did the cleaning."

He frowned, confused. He glanced at Christine before saying to me, "Are you the police?"

"No, Martin," Christine answered. "They just came to talk to me about Emily."

"Oh. Sad." He shoved a hand in his pocket. "I won't need to come back until the regular cleaning at four."

"That's fine."

"It was just a busted pipe."

"Okay."

We watched him leave. I looked at Rosemary. She rolled her eyes.

"He's a nice young man," Christine said.

Rosemary made a noise.

"He doesn't seem too smart, it's true, but he's bright in his own way. He loves animals. He has tattoos on both arms of a raccoon, a deer's head, a fish, and a raven. I see them when he wears their regular uniform with the short-sleeved shirts."

"I see," I said, not really seeing the connection between tattoos of animals and being nice. Or bright.

"Everyone here has been very supportive. Dr. Stevenson has been phenomenal."

I stood up. "Thanks for your time, Mrs. Clement."

"It's all right. I just wish I could have been some help."

CHAPTER

Nineteen

As we were leaving the building, we bumped into Patrick, who was just coming out of the main floor lab office. Tucking his health card into his wallet, he grinned when he saw us.

"Nick and Nora! What are you two doing here?"

"We were talking to the mother of Emily Clement," I said.

We walked together outside into the parking lot. "Really. How did that go?"

I shrugged.

His eyebrows went up. "Hey, have you two had lunch yet? Come on over to the office with me. I'll get sandwiches delivered and you can tell me about it."

"No thanks," Rosemary said.

He smiled. "Free food."

She looked at me. I said, "Thanks, Patrick. We'll see you there."

In the Escalade, as I drove past Patrick on his bicycle and headed back downtown, Rosemary made a face. "I don't like him."

"You don't like anyone," I said.

"Yes I do. I like you, even though you're rich and all your friends are rich."

I digested this for half a block. "Okay, so why don't you like Patrick?"

"Because he's rich. You can tell by the clothes he wears. And the shoes. Designer stuff all the way."

I decided not to point out the obvious contradiction in what she'd just said about me and what she was now saying about Patrick. "Don't you think you're prejudging him based on his economic status and not on the kind of person he is?"

"No."

We pulled into the municipal parking lot across the street from Patrick's building. By some miracle, I found a vacant spot and claimed it just ahead of a cruising pickup truck. I shut off the engine.

"Let me tell you a little bit about him. Maybe it'll change your mind."

"Maybe not."

"Anyway. Yes, he comes from a well-off family. His father, Sean Dillon, is a vice-president with one of the big publishing companies in Toronto, and his mother's a doctor. An internist."

She folded her arms, satisfied that I'd just proven her point for her.

"He got his undergraduate degree at Ryerson; four years. Some of it was paid for by small grants and bursaries that he earned with his high grades, but most of it, plus all his living expenses, was paid off with money he earned cleaning toilets and emptying trash cans at the train station downtown."

She said nothing.

"Not a dime came from his parents. He wouldn't accept it."

She unclipped her seat belt.

"He worked that disgusting job for four years, full-time in the summer and part-time during the school year. After that, he earned enough money writing freelance to pay his way through grad school, so someone else finally replaced him cleaning the toilets. He's a great young man. I think you should cut him some slack."

She got out of the Escalade. I followed, and we jaywalked across the road and trudged up to the offices of the *Sentinel*.

Patrick was already in his office, sitting in front of his computer. "Food's on the way. I'm just looking at the layout for the next issue. Tonight's our copy deadline."

Rosemary and I sat down.

"I've written a follow-up story on Nathan." He clicked on something with his mouse. "I interviewed Grace this morning." He pawed around in the mess on his desk and pulled out a five-by-seven photograph. "She gave me this picture of him. It's okay, but I was wondering if you'd do another illustration for me."

"Sure," I said. "When would you like it?"

"How about right now?"

"Right now?"

"Look, I know you've been giving me a hometown discount, and I appreciate it, but I made some calls and I'm embarrassed, frankly. We sold a bunch of extra full-page ads for this week, so I'm willing to pay you the going rate this time. And from now on, whenever I can."

"It's not about the money, Patrick."

"Not enough time? You couldn't do something while we're talking?"

"Well, yeah, but . . ."

He lunged at his printer and handed me some paper. "I don't have a clipboard, but how about this?"

He pulled out a slim hardcover book from underneath a stack of magazines: *School's Out: A Pictorial History of Ontario's Converted Schoolhouses*, by Anne M. Logan. "Sure, but—"

He held out a ballpoint pen.

I shook my head. "Do you have a grease pencil?"

"A China marker? Yeah, around here somewhere."

He pulled out a drawer and shuffled around in it. "Here we go."

"Thanks." I glanced at the photograph of Nathan, slid a piece of paper on top of the book, and began to sketch.

"You better not have upset Grace," Rosemary said, glaring at Patrick.

"I didn't. She was fine. I didn't stay very long."

"I don't want her being harassed like this."

"Rosemary, it was fine. I know how to talk to people who are under a lot of emotional strain." He shrugged. "It's what I do."

"Do you have a number six pencil?" I asked.

He ransacked the drawer again and produced a tin of Faber-Castell pencils. I took the one I wanted and began to add some shading to the drawing.

Closing the drawer, Patrick said, "How was Mrs. Clement?"

Rosemary shrugged. "I don't know. What can you say? She was sad."

"I've never met her. Dorothy Kerr covered the story for me. What's she like?"

Rosemary didn't respond for a moment. "Tired," she finally said. "Worn out. She's had her ass kicked by life and yet she gets up the next morning and goes back for more."

I handed Patrick the sketch, thinking that Nathan had been a handsome young man, much like Dr. MacPherson. Dark hair; hazel eyes; firm jaw. Only the scar on his left temple that disappeared up into his uneven hairline betrayed the horrible accident that had changed his life.

"Holy cow. In one take. Incredible. Thank you, Mark."

"Are you sure that's what you want? I can do a few more, if you like."

"This is it." He grabbed a file folder, dumped out its contents, and put the sketch in it. "Perfect. Thanks."

Someone knocked on the doorframe. "Did you order food, Patrick?"

A man walked in carrying several paper bags. Patrick cleared a space on the corner of his desk. "Thanks, Kip."

"No problem. I saw it was prepaid, but I gave the guy a tip anyway out of petty cash."

"Good. Thanks. Kip, you know Mark Heron. And this is Rosemary, uh. . . ."

"Nolan."

"Hey, Rosemary, good to meet you. I'm Kip Benson. I'm the sales guy around here."

"Kip got us those extra ads that'll pay for your illustration, Mark."

I gave him a two-fingered salute. "Much appreciated."

"You betcha." He left the room as Patrick opened one of the bags.

"Okay, I've got roast beef on rye here, and, uh, chicken salad sandwich. Rosemary?"

"Anything else?"

He grabbed the other bag. "Let's see. BLT and ham and cheese."

"BLT."

"Mark?"

"Chicken."

"Nice. You left me the roast beef. My favourite."

He opened up the final bag. "Iced tea, Coke, and ginger ale."

"Coke," Rosemary said. She took the can from him. "Thanks."

"Mark?"

"Iced tea."

"And ginger ale for me. So I went through the notes one more time that Dorothy put on file after the Emily story ran, and nothing is jumping out." He took a bite of his sandwich.

"I don't think I know her," I said. "Kerr?"

Patrick swallowed and took a shot of his drink. "Freelancer, as I said, but really very good. And experienced. I'm going to hire her full time as soon as I can manage it."

Rosemary frowned but said nothing, concentrating on her sandwich.

We chewed and swallowed and slurped in silence for a few minutes.

"I think I may have another talk with Mrs. Clement myself," Patrick said. "See if she mentions something new. That she never thought of before."

"Help yourself," Rosemary said, "but you'll just be wasting your breath. A year's a long time ago, and she's probably blocked out a lot of it by now, anyway."

"You could be right."

"This article on Nathan," I said. "Will you be making a connection to the other missing persons whose names have come up? Emily and the other two?"

"Not right now. I thought I'd see if the story would generate something specific on Nathan himself for starters." He glanced at Rosemary. "Doesn't mean I don't think there may be a connection, though."

"What about the OPP?" I asked.

Patrick nodded. "The regular guy, Shepard, wasn't available, so I talked to a Detective Constable Barnes. 'No developments at this time, but the investigation is ongoing.' Quote unquote."

"Christ," Rosemary muttered.

Patrick didn't hear her. He was gazing at the ceiling, his last bite of sandwich forgotten in his hand. I glanced at Rosemary, but she was staring at her can of Coke.

"That's a good idea," Patrick suddenly said. He began pawing through the stuff on his desk, then reached into his back pocket and pulled out his cellphone.

"I should have thought of this before."

I watched him open his Contacts list, scroll down, and punch a name.

"Hey," he said when the call was answered. "It's Patrick. How are you doing, Dorothy?"

He listened for a moment, a smile curling the corners of his mouth. "Good. Look, I have a quick question for you, and it's a bit of a memory teaser."

He nodded. "Yeah, I know. Okay. You remember the story you covered for me about the missing woman, Emily Clement?"

He listened for a moment. "Right. Yeah, you're not kidding. Anyway, I'm taking another look at it—sure, that's all right, I understand; I'm going to cover it myself—yeah, I'm trying to remember something you told me at the time that didn't go into your notes."

He closed his eyes and tipped back his head. "No, it was just a detail we didn't bother with at the time. Did you, or did you not, tell me that when you interviewed Mrs.

Clement, someone was there with her at the house?"

He smiled as he listened. "Right, that's it. The brother. Uh huh? Okay, that's why his name isn't in the notes. Right. Did you ever get an address for him?"

Patrick swivelled in his chair and grabbed the ballpoint pen I'd turned down. He flipped over a sheet of paper and began scribbling. "Uh huh. Uh huh. Anything else? No, that's great. Listen, one other thing."

He laughed. "No, you passed the memory test. That was it. I was wondering if you'd be interested in coming on full strength with me here. I think I can find the money in the budget and—"

He snapped his fingers. "Just like that. Can you come in this week so we can talk it over? I'll make you an offer you can't refuse."

He scribbled something else. "Perfect. I'll be here in the office. Yep. See you then."

He ended the call and pumped his fist. "Great. Outstanding. Should have done that a long time ago."

"Emily Clement?" Rosemary prompted. "Earth to Patrick?"

He blinked at her. "What? Yeah! There's an uncle, a Philip Sampson. Apparently that's Christine's maiden name. Sampson. Anyway, he was there when Dorothy interviewed her, but he didn't want to say anything. Wouldn't go on the record with her, not even for a support-ive statement, and wouldn't go off the record, either. Insisted that she not even write his name down."

"Did you get his address?" I asked.

"No, but he owns a dollar store franchise in the mall. She thought we might track him down there."

Rosemary jumped to her feet. "What the hell are we waiting for? Let's rock."

CHAPTER

Twenty

I happen to like dollar stores. The particular chain Philip Sampson had invested in was one of my favourites. They seemed to specialize in liquidated lots, and I'd had a fair bit of luck finding quality items at a low price. For example, there wasn't another store in town that sold Gold Toe men's hosiery, so why order online and pay for shipping when Dollar Magic suddenly stocks a whole load of them at $1.50 a pair?

We asked for Sampson, and the woman at the cash paged him on the loudspeaker. While we waited, I browsed the pencils and permanent markers but didn't see anything worth buying. Next time in, though, I'd probably pick up a few new sketchbooks.

"Yes, Marcie? What is it?"

Sampson was tall and wide-hipped, with pleasant features and a drastically receding hairline. He wore a short-sleeved white shirt, a red tie, and brown polyester trousers.

"He looks like Richard Deacon," I murmured to

Rosemary.

"Who the hell's that?"

"These people wanted to talk to you," Marcie said, pointing us out.

"I'm Patrick Dillon," Patrick said, holding out his hand. "This is Mark Heron and Rosemary Nolan. Could we have a moment of your time?"

He shook our hands. Rosemary declined. "What's this about? I'm a little busy."

"It's about your niece, Emily Clement."

"What is it? Has she been found? Are you the police?"

"Is there somewhere we can talk in private?"

He led us through the store to a little door at the back corner. It opened into a small office. Sampson sat down behind his desk. There was one visitor's chair. Patrick looked at Rosemary, politely inviting the female in our group to sit down. She looked at me, brusquely inviting the old geezer in our group to sit down. I looked at Patrick and rolled my eyes.

He sat down and took out his notebook but didn't open it. "Mr. Sampson, I'm the publisher of the *Sentinel*. Mr. Heron and Ms. Nolan are helping me with a story that involves Emily, your missing niece. We'd like to ask you a few questions."

I closed the door behind us.

He leaned back abruptly. "You're not the police."

"No, sir. We're not."

"Then go fish. I've got work to do."

"It's my understanding you were with your sister the day Emily disappeared. I—"

"There's the door. Use it."

Patrick paused for a moment, fingering his notebook but leaving it closed. "I'd rather talk to you on the record than off, because I think you might have information that could help us in the search for Emily and another missing person, Nathan Notwell."

"Nope."

"I'll attribute the information to an anonymous source with knowledge of the situation. I won't write down your name," he tapped his notebook with a fingernail, "and I certainly won't mention it in the article."

"Not interested."

"Your niece was how old? Thirty-five?"

Sampson looked away.

"Did you not like her, Mr. Sampson? Was there something about her that bothered you?"

He made a face. "She was fine. What the hell are you talking about?"

"I'm wondering why you refused to talk to my reporter on the scene last year, and why you're refusing to talk to us now. I'm trying to understand the issue."

"There's no issue. I just don't want to talk about it."

"Okay." Patrick pursed his lips, thinking. "What kind of a person was she?"

"I don't know what you're getting at."

"Did she have marital problems? Did she drink? Was she bad tempered?"

"No, of course not. She was a good person. Always good to her mother."

I watched Patrick's face and saw the creases form at the corners of his eyes. He'd broken through, even though it might be just a little bit. "What about booze? Or drugs?"

He shook his head. "She liked a beer now and again, just like all of us. But it wasn't a problem. And no drugs. Not at all."

"She and her husband were divorced, weren't they?"

"This is none of your business."

"It's just a background question, Mr. Sampson. I'm trying to understand her situation."

He thought about it before saying, "Legally, they were only just separated."

"I see. What can you tell me about him?"

"Julian? He was okay. He came out of the closet during one of their fights. Said his boyfriend had just moved out west and he was going to go out there to join him."

"Where out west?"

"Edmonton, I think. Emily was blown away."

"She didn't know anything about it beforehand?"

"She sure as hell didn't."

"Have you or Christine heard anything from him since? Maybe asking about Emily?"

Sampson shook his head. "Nope. I'm done talking about this. Please leave."

Patrick leaned forward. "Just a few—"

"No. Beat it. Or I'll call the cops myself and have you thrown out."

I straightened up. "Thanks for your time."

Following my cue, Patrick tapped his notebook on his knee and got to his feet. Rosemary was already opening the office door.

We walked down to the bank at the end of the mall. Patrick sat down on a bench, flipped open his notebook, and began to scribble.

"I don't like that guy," Rosemary said.

I sat down on the end of the bench next to Patrick. My back was a little sore from having stood so long in the cramped quarters of Sampson's office.

"Why not?" I was being sarcastic, but she didn't catch it.

"I don't know. He gives me the creeps."

"Think he's hiding something?"

"He's hiding a ton," Patrick said. "We just have to figure out what."

CHAPTER

Twenty-One

That evening someone rang my doorbell a few minutes before eight o'clock. I opened the door and looked at a heavy-set man in a tan jacket over a yellow and brown Hawaiian shirt, brown denim pants, and brown walking shoes. I knew without having to be told that he was a cop, but he held up his wallet anyway to show his warrant card and badge.

"Detective Constable Shepard, OPP. Are you Mark Heron?"

"Yes, I am." I looked over his shoulder at an unmarked charcoal grey Charger that was parked behind my Escalade.

"May I come in? I have a few questions for you."

It seemed to be the day for interviews, and now it appeared I would be on the receiving end.

"Sure. Come on in." I led the way through the living room into the solarium where we could watch the sun settle down below the treeline. "Can I get you something? Coffee? Cold drink?"

"No. This won't take long."

I sat down but he remained on his feet, putting his hands on his hips. The movement brushed the edges of his jacket aside, allowing me a glimpse of his holstered sidearm.

Uh oh, I thought. He's going to be rolling out the Howitzers any time now.

"I'll get right to the point. I understand you've involved yourself in a case I'm investigating, and I'd like to know why."

"If you're referring to the disappearance of Nathan Notwell—"

"What's your interest in him?"

"I'm trying to help a friend, Rosemary Nolan. She's a friend of his mother."

"How long have you known this Nolan girl?"

"Only a short while. She saw an illustration of mine in the *Sentinel* and thought it was Nathan. She came around to ask me about it."

"And was it?"

I frowned. "Sorry?"

"Was it a picture of Nathan Notwell?"

"No, no. I explained to her it was something I'd done during the Gulf War. A doctor I met in a Canadian field hospital while I was embedded there, in ninety-one."

"I see."

I caught his expression. He didn't believe me.

"I can show you the original. It's in my files."

"You live alone here," he said, changing the subject.

"Yes."

"Have many visitors?"

"Yes, occasionally. Did Detective Barnes tell you about us talking to him on Saturday? About Tom O'Toole?"

"What were you doing bothering O'Toole?"

I was getting progressively more upset at his line of

questioning. What the hell was going on? Was he treating me as a suspect for some unknown reason?

"Would you please sit down? I'm starting to get a cramp in my neck looking up at you."

"Please answer the question, Mr. Heron."

Okay, fine. We were going to be on even terms, physically speaking, come hell or high water, so I stood up and put my own hands on my hips.

"We weren't bothering him, Detective. As we explained to your colleague, we learned that Nathan liked to walk along the river with a young friend who was afraid of an old man who lived down there under the bridge. We went down there to question him about Nathan's disappearance."

"You don't need to be questioning anyone. O'Toole's already known to us. He's not a sex offender or a threat to anyone. He's a homeless person who lost his family in a car crash eight years ago. He worked in one of the banks in town but already had mental health issues and was getting treatment when the accident happened. We keep an eye on him to make sure he's okay, but we don't take official notice of him because then we'd have to move him out from under that bridge. We'd rather just let sleeping dogs lie for right now. He stays out of trouble. That's his story. Now, what's yours?"

"I'm afraid I don't understand. I don't have a story."

"You live alone; you have no family; you've inserted yourself into an investigation to which you have no obvious connection; and you won't explain why. You can answer my questions here, or at the detachment office. Your choice."

I was stunned. He *was* treating me like a suspect. "Do I need to call a lawyer?"

"I don't know. Do you?"

Rubbing my forehead, I sat down again and gestured to

a chair. "Please."

Thankfully, he sat down this time.

"Yes, I've been divorced for several decades and, yes, I live alone. Rosemary reacted to the illustration and came to see me. I told her that if it was something being investigated by the police, I didn't see where there was anything I could do. She . . . kind of talked me into giving a damn, I guess. We talked to Nathan's cousin, Grace. It was very sad. After we talked to the old man, O'Toole, we came to the detachment office looking for you, but you weren't there."

"Anything else you'd like to get off your chest?"

Frustration flared inside me. "Yeah, actually. Did you make a connection between Nathan's disappearance and Emily Clement's disappearance last August?"

"There isn't one."

"I'm not so sure. What about Lucy Banner and Peter Forrest? Are they connected?"

He stared at me for a long moment. "What do you know about them?"

"Essentially nothing, but it's starting to feel like the same person might be responsible in each case."

"What makes you say that, Mr. Heron? Personal knowledge?"

"Of course not! Don't be absurd. If you think I kidnapped Nathan and these other people, you're eating the wrong kind of Wheaties for breakfast. This thing's starting to pull me in because I care, because the families are breaking my heart, and the thought of these people having been victimized by a maniac who's getting away with it is making me feel more and more frustrated with each passing day. I'd like to think you'd take seriously the idea that there's more to this than meets the eye."

"I take everything seriously, Mr. Heron. You can count on that." He stood up. "I'll be in touch."

That was it. He walked out, got into his car, and drove away.

I stood at the front door for the longest time, trying to get a grip on my raging emotions.

Under suspicion?

It was intolerable.

CHAPTER

Twenty-Two

I didn't get much sleep that night. Shepard's visit had shaken me to the core. How could someone think that I was the kind of person who would harm another human being, let alone be responsible for their disappearance and possible death? It was horrible. Unthinkable.

The next morning I moped around the house, catching up on housework and watering the houseplants. Feeling vulnerable and sorry for myself, I suppose.

After fixing myself a hearty lunch, I retreated to the studio and worked on the Halloween gags. This time the dark wash behaved, and by the end of the afternoon I was able to send them off to the magazine.

Exhausted, I spent the evening watching television, went to bed early, read for a while, then caught up on some badly needed sleep.

When I was a kid, I used to walk a lot. I'd walk from one end of Cobourg to the other and back again. I'd walk to music lessons (violin: I was terrible), I'd walk to my girlfriend's house, I'd walk to the beach. All that walking stuck in my head over the years, so that I frequently dreamed about walking. Dreams can be very stream-of-consciousness things as our mind digests occurrences from our waking hours, and more often than not something that happened to me during the day would provide an objective to which I had to walk that night in my sleep. I'd pass a lot of people along the way, who mostly ignored me, and I'd keep on going until the dream morphed into something entirely different.

Occasionally I'd be lost. I was supposed to meet up with someone or find something, but the streets and buildings became unfamiliar and confusing, and I'd be upset. Walking and walking, and not arriving. A definite fear of failure as the underlying theme of the dream. I still remember one that I had many years ago, when I was a young man, in which I was supposed to be playing goaltender for the Montreal Canadiens but I was up in the press box because my mother wanted to tell me something and she wasn't there yet. The game had started without me and no one was playing goal, and the announcer kept saying, "He scores! He scores! He scores!"

Fear of failure.

Sometimes I was trying to get away from something or someone that was threatening me. These ones often had a supernatural overtone, where I felt that something shadowy and evil was relentlessly stalking me. It was this kind that I had on this particular night, and when I woke up at twenty past three in the morning, I dismissed it as the usual fear of impending death. The unpleasant encounter with Shepard had definitely sent me into sleep in a dark mood, and my imagination had taken care of the rest.

It took a while for me to be able to read myself back to the land of Nod.

The following day, Wednesday, I hit the studio early

and spent the day working. There was no possible way I was going to leave the house other than to take my daily walk around the property, so I decided the best thing would be to keep busy on what I knew best.

I hit my library of cartoon books, looking for examples of police humour, but I couldn't find what I was looking for, so I sat down at the drawing board with a cup of coffee and started to doodle.

Uniformed cop on the beat with his hands on his hips, looking down at a bag lady with an innocent-looking expression on her face and a ray gun sticking out of her shopping cart. Caption: "What little green man?"

Ugh.

Man in a goofy-looking goat suit sitting on a chair under the bright lights while a detective loomed over him, hands on hips. Caption: "I swear, I never saw that tin can before in my life!"

Pffthhtt.

I tried a few more, hoping for a cathartic effect by working out the fear and frustrations Shepard had caused, but the Muse wasn't talking to me today.

I dashed off a couple of man-on-a-desert-island gags, always a good port in a storm, pun intended, and then quit for the day.

That night, thankfully, I slept fairly well, without dreams that woke me up at three in the morning. After breakfast I puttered around in the kitchen, pickling some small cucumbers with dill, garlic, and salt, and then left the pail to soak as I went for my usual walk.

I was just coming back through the yard behind the house when I heard the growl of Rosemary's Harley in the driveway. I went around the side of the house and was surprised to see Patrick dismounting from the passenger seat behind her.

"Oh man," he said, yanking off his helmet, "that was unbelievable." He pointed to the seat. "Did you know they call this the pillion? I saw it online. It's from a Scottish Gaelic word, referring to small pelts they put on a horse for a second rider to sit on. Cool, eh?"

"Hello, Patrick."

"What? Yeah! Hello! Man, I'd forgotten how exhilarating it is. I used to tool around with a high school pal of mine who had an old Triumph, but this is just incredible!"

"I think I've created a monster," Rosemary said as she walked past me toward the verandah.

"Would you prefer sitting inside or outside?"

"Outside."

I pointed. "Let's go around the back onto the patio."

She detoured away from the verandah and led the way around the side of the house.

Patrick held out a newspaper. "The story's running."

"I'm not sure I want to stay involved."

He stared at me. "Why not?"

I got them settled on the patio, took beverage orders, and went inside. A Coke for Rosemary, no glass; a ginger ale for Patrick, in a glass with a slice of lime; and a bourbon on the rocks for me.

When everyone was settled, I sat down and pulled on my drink. "I'm not comfortable with all this right now."

"Why the hell not?" Rosemary glared at me. "We're just starting to make some progress, and now you're weaselling out on us?"

"I'm not weaselling out." Another swallow. "Detective Shepard came around on Monday."

"So? He talked to me, too."

"Did he?" I raised my eyebrows. "Did he treat you like

a suspect?"

"No, of course not. Wait. What are you saying?"

"He made it clear I was near the top of his list."

"You're kidding."

"I kid you not."

"That's fucking absurd," Rosemary growled. "You're the kindest, most gentle old git I've ever met in my life. He's full of shit."

"Thanks, I guess."

"I don't get it," Patrick frowned. "What'd he say?"

"He applied the usual profile, I guess. Lives alone; no family; and I've inserted myself into the investigation. Classic serial predator behaviour, apparently."

Rosemary thumped her Coke can. "I *told* him about the old guy down at the river. He said they had nothing on him, that he wasn't a suspect. Like, what the hell?"

"Did you tell him about Philip Sampson? That we think he knows more about Emily's disappearance than he's letting on? And he should look into a possible connection to Nathan and the other missing persons?"

"I didn't get a chance, the rammy bastard. He warned me not to interfere and buggered off."

We both looked at Patrick.

"I didn't talk to him."

"You'll have to read the story," Rosemary said to me, shifting gears. "Grace told him something about a truck."

"A truck?"

Patrick still had the paper in his hand. He put it down on the table in front of me. It was folded to the story he'd written about Nathan.

I was relieved to see that the illustration I'd given him looked great. I started to read the article, but Patrick interrupted.

"I'll save you the trouble," he said. "Grace mentioned something about a black pickup truck around the park that had bothered Nathan. I take it she didn't mention it to you before."

I looked at Rosemary. "Not when I was there. Rosemary?"

"Nope. News to me."

"What about this truck?" I asked.

"It was just something in passing. We were talking about whether or not she worried about the safety of her children, living here in town. She said she hadn't before Nathan disappeared. He'd mentioned one time that he'd seen a man looking at him while driving past the park in a black pickup truck, but when the guy saw that Nathan was looking at him he drove away."

"Did she mention it to the police?"

"She said she didn't think it was important enough at the time, and after Nathan's disappearance she'd forgotten about it and it fell through the cracks. That's why I included it in the story."

"Now you'll probably hear from Shepard."

He shrugged. "I'll bet he's already aware of it."

"And doing jack shit about it, as usual," Rosemary groused.

Patrick looked at me. "I'm going to talk to Nathan's boss and co-workers at the factory. I'd like you to come with me, Mark."

"I don't know." I was unwilling to incur the further wrath of Detective Constable Shepard.

"You can't weasel out now," Rosemary said.

A life without risk is a life without reward, I thought.

"All right."

CHAPTER

Twenty-Three

Monica Palmer was a tall, wide-hipped woman in her fifties with carefully maintained blond hair, a lantern jaw, and friendly blue eyes. She met us inside the main entrance of the Palmer Woollen Goods Company on Campbell Street, down at the river.

"Thanks for seeing us," Patrick said. "I hope we're not interrupting something important."

"It's fine. I'll take you back to Nathan's work area." She led us through a large space filled with noisy machinery to a stock room lined with shelves. I stared at a dizzying array of products in all colours and sizes, neatly stacked and identified by barcodes and stock-keeping unit (SKU) numbers. She noticed the look on my face and smiled.

"Impressive, isn't it? I'm proud of our little company."

"You seem to be doing well," Patrick said, peeking around the corner of a shelving unit at another aisle racked with product.

"That's an understatement," Monica said, her voice betraying a faint British accent. "Wool's an odd commodity. Because of COVID and the global disruptions it caused, producers saw the demand for wool drop, which lowered prices significantly. I'm told that 30 per cent of the wool that was produced during the pandemic failed to sell, and in some regions in Canada up to 50 per cent went unused. A lot of it got composted, which is a shame."

"You seem to be putting it to good use," Patrick remarked.

"Yes, we are. In the past we processed the wool, buying it raw and carding it, spinning it, dyeing it, the whole thing. Now we buy whatever we want already finished, and we manufacture the goods right here to sell to our clientele. Blankets, sweaters, socks, skirts, mittens, hats—you name it. Much more cost effective this way."

She led us through a doorway into another large room that was set up for packing and shipping orders.

"This is Sheila," she said, indicating a young brunette who stood at a long table taping up a shipping carton. "We brought her in to replace Nathan."

Sheila glanced over her shoulder at us as she set aside her tape gun and removed a set of labels from a small printer.

"As you can see," Monica continued, "each order is displayed on this eighty-five-inch screen above the work station. Each item is shown with the correct size and colour requested by the customer. Sheila takes her hand basket to the stock room, picks the order, double checks that everything's correct, prints out the invoice and the labels, packs and seals the carton, labels it, and places it in here for pickup in the morning." She indicated a large plastic bin on wheels.

"Very impressive," Patrick said. "I'd like to send someone around later to do a profile on you, if you wouldn't mind."

"That would be nice."

"Today, though, we want to talk to you about Nathan. How did you happen to hire him, Mrs. Palmer?"

"It was through the Community Services people, actually. When our previous picker left, I contacted them to see if they might have someone. I've hired people through them before, you see, and it's always worked out quite well."

"And did Nathan? Work out well?"

"Oh, yes. He's a very good-natured person, always friendly to his co-workers. A little shy and withdrawn. I understand he endured some bullying at the group therapy sessions that upset him, but I was told they straightened that out before he . . . disappeared."

"Did his disability affect his work?"

She smiled. "No, that was a pleasant surprise. I understood that his injury had left him with some cognitive impairment and memory problems, but that's where my son John stepped in. He handles all our IT needs, and Nathan's arrival gave him the opportunity to develop this program you see up there on the big board. It was a project he'd had in mind for a while, and Nathan was the perfect test subject. With the entire order up there on the screen, Nathan easily learned the simple steps required to pick the orders and check them off in the system as they went into the carton. John was extremely pleased with the outcome."

"You mentioned problems at the group therapy sessions," I said. "Were there any here?"

"Absolutely not. I wouldn't stand for it." She folded her arms. "I employ a dozen people here, not counting John, and during the run-up to Christmas I add at least a half dozen more. I interview everyone myself. Personal suitability and interpersonal skills are at the top of my list of requirements. No one ever bothered or upset Nathan while he was here, or else I would have heard about it immediately and taken action."

I nodded. "Did you ever notice anyone hanging around, maybe out in the parking lot or visiting your storefront?"

"No. The police went through all this with me before. There's nothing I can add to what I told them."

"Are you aware that there have been other disappearances in town over the past year or so?"

"Heavens, no."

"Lucy Banner, a music teacher. Emily Clement, a librarian. Peter Forrest, a high school senior."

"I don't know any of these people. You're saying they disappeared as well?"

"Within the last year."

"This is terrible. Do you think they're connected?"

"That's what we're looking into now," Patrick said.

"But what about the police? What do they think?"

"They don't," Rosemary murmured.

"They don't believe there's a connection right now," Patrick said, as though completing Rosemary's sentence.

"But you do?"

"We think there's a possibility. We want to know more."

"If I can help in any way, Patrick, please let me know."

"I will," he said, closing his notebook.

Outside, we stood around Rosemary's bike and talked it over. It seemed very unlikely that Nathan's abductor had been one of his co-workers. The police would have already covered this possibility, and Mrs. Palmer was very convincing. I believed without question that if someone working for the Palmer Woollen Goods Company had meant Nathan any harm, she would have been on top of it in a heartbeat.

"I don't think there's any point in interviewing her employees," Patrick said.

"I agree." I pulled out my key fob. "What's next?"

"Fuck."

We both looked at Rosemary, who was staring at a black pickup truck parked at the curb across the street.

"He's watching us," she muttered.

Sure enough, I saw the man behind the steering wheel of the truck lower a pair of binoculars and turn away. The truck's engine roared.

"Shit!" Rosemary shouted. "Hey you!" She jumped onto her bike and gunned it into life just as the truck pulled away from the curb and took off down the street.

I smacked Patrick on the shoulder. "Come on!"

We raced to the Escalade and hurried after them.

The truck ran a stop sign and Rosemary followed, slowly gaining ground. I slowed a little to make sure the intersection was clear before running it as well.

At the next corner, the truck fishtailed right onto Perry Street. Rosemary jumped the curb, cut across the corner of someone's lawn, and landed only a couple of meters behind him. The Harley's engine roared. I slowed, turned, and saw that they were already approaching the intersection of Gore Street, where traffic would be heavier.

I saw the truck's brake lights flare, and it swerved left onto Gore, narrowly avoiding an oncoming car. Rosemary hit the sidewalk to avoid another car, then bounced onto the street, still behind the truck. I braked at the intersection to allow two cars to pass.

"You're good this way!" Patrick shouted, caught up in the excitement of the chase.

Breathless with fear, heart pounding, I hit a gap and turned left onto Gore. Ahead of us, the light was green at the next intersection. I watched the truck turn right. Rosemary stayed right on his tail. As I approached the corner, the light turned yellow. I whipped the steering wheel around and we skidded onto New Scotland Road, not far behind them.

We drove this way for about a kilometer, leaving the town limits behind us, a caravan of three. Suddenly up ahead I saw a line of traffic stopped at a railway crossing. The truck's lights came on as the driver slowed. He edged over onto the shoulder, then back out across the centre line, but there were no options available to him. A train was passing, with no end in sight. He slowed. Stopped.

Rosemary gunned the bike around his back end, fishtailed, killed the engine, and hopped off. I pulled up behind them as she climbed up on the truck's running board and pounded on the driver's window.

"Get out of the truck! Get out of the fucking truck!"

I stopped and jumped out. Patrick was several strides ahead of me. He grabbed Rosemary and tried to pull her down from the running board, but she held onto the side mirror with one hand and kept pounding with the other.

"Get out of there, you son of a bitch! Get out!"

The driver of the car ahead of us came back to see what was going on. He was a young guy with messy hair and a pencil moustache. "What's up with the chick? She gone nuts or something?"

"Call 911," I told him.

"Sure, man."

At that point Patrick succeeded in detaching Rosemary from the side mirror. When he pulled, she fell down onto the pavement, rear end and elbows banging hard. Cursing, she sprang back up again and lunged at the truck.

"Where's Nathan? What have you done with him, you son of a bitch?"

Patrick wrapped her in a bear hug and whispered in her ear. She struggled.

The driver of the truck lowered his window a crack. "What's your problem? Are you fucking insane? Go away!"

They went back and forth, exchanging shouts, until an OPP cruiser showed up, light bar flashing, and a uniformed officer took charge of the mess.

CHAPTER

Twenty-Four

This time I sat by myself in a different interview room at the detachment office, one with a table bolted to the floor and two chairs, one for the detective and the other for the interviewee. A camera in the corner of the ceiling was pointed at me, the little red light turned on, and when Detective Constable Ed Barnes came in and sat down, he flicked a switch on the microphone on the table and moved it closer to me.

Total A-V coverage. On the record.

"You're lucky you get me and not Shepard," he said after we'd completed the preliminaries of legal rights and warnings and so on. "He's some pissed."

"I'm really sorry," I said. "This whole thing has gotten out of hand."

"You're telling me. He's reading your girlfriend the riot act right now."

"She's not my girlfriend. She's young enough to be my granddaughter."

He just stared at me. I suddenly thought of the age difference between Bob Champion and May, and felt my face grow warm.

"Look, pop, you're way out of your depth. Why don't you just walk me through what you were doing at the factory and why you were racing around town like a crazy idiot."

I explained the meeting with Mrs. Palmer and our questions about Nathan. I asked him if he'd read Patrick's article on Nathan's disappearance, in which Grace had mentioned a black pickup truck that had upset him. He hadn't. I tried to describe the shock and surprise we'd felt at seeing the same black truck outside the woollen mill, but it sounded lame even to my ears.

"How'd you know it was the same truck?"

"Um. I guess we didn't, exactly."

"You just assumed it was and took off after the guy."

"Well . . ."

"You know what happens when you assume."

I knew the old joke—you make an ass of you and me. "Yeah."

"Okay. So, did you see your girlfriend hit Mr. Follett at any time?"

"No, she did not."

"Did you see her strike his vehicle at any time?"

"No, other than pounding on his window to get him to lower it."

"Did you hear her threaten him at any time?"

"No. She didn't threaten him. She wanted to know what he'd done with Nathan."

"And did Mr. Follett at any time make any statement to suggest he knew what she was talking about? Did he say anything at all about Nathan Notwell, missing persons, or anything else to lead you to believe you were on the right track by chasing this guy all around town like some crazed fool?"

"No. He did not." I sighed. "What was he doing there, if he wasn't stalking us, trying to figure out if we were getting close to him?"

Barnes leaned back and tapped the table lightly with his hand. "Mr. Heron. What can I say? You need to go home and keep your nose out of stuff that isn't your business. But if it'll get you to back off, Ian Follett's daughter Sheila works at Palmer. He was trying to see her through the windows."

"I don't understand."

"There's a restraining order against him. Part of the divorce. He has to stay away from the kid, which he has a hard time doing. This is the second time he's been caught violating the order."

"So that's why he took off when we asked what he was doing?"

Barnes spread his hands.

I slumped in the chair, defeated.

"Beat it," Barnes told me. "Get out of here before Shepard catches sight of you and decides to hit you with an obstruction charge. Stay out of shit that doesn't concern you."

I nodded.

He opened the door.

I left.

CHAPTER

Twenty-Five

The following morning I woke up to the sound of thunder. I opened my eyes and stared at the ceiling, listening to heavy rain pounding on the tin roof and against the window panes. Lightning flashed through the half-drawn curtains and I counted—one steamboat, two steamboats, three steamboats—and thunder rumbled across the sky again.

If I remembered correctly, a three-second interval meant the lightning strike was about a kilometer away. Fairly close.

I showered, dressed, and ate a slow breakfast of buttered toast and coffee in the kitchen. I had a solid rule against going for my daily walk during a thunderstorm, as it was a risky proposition given the tree cover around the place and the possibility that lightning would pose a safety hazard, so I decided I'd wait until later in the day to see if the storm abated.

I didn't mind walking when it was wet, since that's what rain gear and Wellingtons were for. It was the lightning that held me back.

I went into the studio and did some tidy-up, filing stuff away and catching up on my account books. I kept track of all my submissions, giving each gag a name, listing the publications I sent them to, which ones were accepted, and when they appeared in print. No one else would do this for me, so I did it myself. It was busywork, but I didn't mind. It kept my thoughts in order, as well as my business.

Close to eleven o'clock the phone rang. I looked at the call display and saw a long-distance number I didn't recognize. It was probably a Revenue Canada fraud call, informing me that I would be sent to prison unless I provided my bank account information immediately or whatever. I usually let that crap ring through, but I was in a mood so I picked up, mayhem in mind.

"Is this Mark Heron?" a woman's voice asked.

"Yeah, I'm here with the *consigliere*. Whadda ya want?"

"Mark, is that you? It's Adrienne O'Neill calling."

I laughed, embarrassed. "Adrienne! Sorry, I thought it was someone else."

"That's all right. It's been a while, hasn't it? Three or four years? How are you doing?"

Adrienne was the art director of *Your Home and Garden*, one of the top-selling magazines in the United States. We went back a long way together, and while I hadn't sent her anything for quite a long time, she remained close to the top of the list of my favourite people in the industry. A wife, mother, and grandmother, she was perhaps the sweetest person I'd ever met.

"I'm well, thank you. Yourself?"

"Knee-deep in grandkids. What can I say? Look, I'm in a bit of a crunch and I was wondering if I could ask a favour."

"For you, anything."

"You're such a darling. I'm in crisis mode right now, and I need help. Our Labour Day issue is about to wrap and I suddenly got word that the cartoons I was going to run are no longer available."

"Uh oh."

"You know Sergio Planck. He just passed away. Massive heart attack."

"My God!" I was shocked. Well known for his editorial cartoons and caricatures, Sergio was a reclusive type whose work was coveted by publications around the world. I myself had three of his collections on the bookshelf behind me.

"I just got a call from a lawyer telling me all his contracts are being pulled," Adrienne went on, her voice high-pitched with stress. "I've got two of his gags in this issue to go along with our cover piece on the history of Labour Day. I need something quick."

"I see."

"You're only semi-retired, right? That's what I heard. If you're not working, don't worry. I'm only partway down my list."

"You mean I wasn't your first call?"

She laughed nervously. "I didn't want to bother you."

"No bother at all. The history of Labour Day, eh?"

"Yes. Can you send me a bundle by six o'clock? Including a cover?"

"You betcha."

"Oh my God, Mark. You're a lifesaver."

We confirmed e-mail addresses, her formatting preferences, and other details. I ended the call and went into the kitchen to make a pot of coffee.

This was why I would never, ever retire. Why I wouldn't

quit drawing gags until they pulled the grease pencil from my cold, dead hand. The spike of adrenaline at a sudden creative challenge was what I lived for. Everything else that had been going wrong was forgotten. My spirits soared, and my mind began buzzing with ideas.

I carried a steaming cup into the studio and went first to my filing cabinet. I had a folder with a dozen or more unsold gags spoofing unions, Labour Day, and related topics. They weren't much good, though, which was why they were here in my "Unsold" drawer rather than in print somewhere out there in the universe.

The best of the lot was a drawing of a guy reclining on a couch watching TV while his wife stands by with her hands on her hips. The caption reads, "Once a year I get a holiday from the endless grind of job-hunting. I wish you'd let me enjoy it in peace."

I hesitated, then pulled it out and put it on the drawing table. It was lame and derivative, but it would serve as a starting point. Returning the folder to the drawer, I grabbed a handful of eight-and-a-half by eleven paper and started scribbling down ideas.

A while later, I got up for more paper. I worked a bit longer and then went into the kitchen to refill my coffee cup. I didn't look at the time, so I had no idea how long I'd been working. I barely paid attention to my surroundings—my head was swirling, rejecting bits, accepting others, visualizing how they would be drawn.

I had four roughs I considered good enough to submit and was working up a fifth when the phone rang. Thinking it might be Adrienne again, I grabbed the studio portable and answered without looking.

"I'm getting there!"

"Mark?"

It was Patrick.

"I've been making some calls," he said, his voice brisk and enthusiastic. "I'm going to go talk to Philip Sampson again, and I wonder if you'd like to come with me."

"Emily Clement's uncle? The dollar store guy?" With all the turmoil and stress generated by the Ian Follett fiasco, I'd forgotten about him.

"Yeah. I think I've come across information that'll give us some leverage on him this time."

"I don't think so."

"Why not, Mark?"

I drew in a long breath. "I've been questioned twice by the police, Patrick. Which I don't like at all. I've been warned to stay away from their investigation on both occasions, and I'm beginning to see their point. Plus, I'm working against a deadline right now. I couldn't possibly leave the studio."

"Okay." He paused for a moment. "How about I bring you up to date?"

"Sure. Why not."

"All right. First, Shepard tried leaning on me pretty heavily, but I wasn't having any of it. I told him as a journalist working on a story, I wasn't going to be intimidated. I started asking *him* questions."

"Good for you."

"He gave me next to nothing, other than the fact that Follett is not considered a suspect in Nathan's disappearance, and I can see where they're coming from, so that's fine. So I switched gears on him and asked him if there were any updates on the Emily Clement disappearance. That was a negative, too."

"I see." I was trying to be polite and pay attention, but my mind was on my work and not on what he was saying.

"So I shifted gears and asked if they'd checked to see whether Philip Sampson had a criminal record. He gave me the usual line about the information in their databases being for police eyes only and off limits to me. I told him I was aware of that, but I wasn't asking about information, I was merely asking if they *checked* for a criminal record. So he said yes, they had. Then he said, 'Why, is your artist friend afraid I was looking him up?' You could have knocked me over with a feather, but I covered my tracks by saying, 'Is that a confirmation that Sampson has a record?' and he just gave me a look."

Patrick had my full attention now. "I don't believe it," I said.

"Yeah, well, don't worry about it, Mark. He was just needling me."

"With all due respect, Patrick, you're not the one he suspects of being a kidnapper. This is very upsetting."

"He doesn't suspect you of being a kidnapper. He's just being a dickhead."

"Jesus."

"Relax. I'm looking at Philip Sampson, remember? The whispers on the wind suggest he has a problem."

"Are you saying *he's* a kidnapper?"

"That's what I'm trying to find out. A friend of his suggested last night that he has serious anger management problems."

"Some friend."

"Yeah. Anyway, I'm going to broach the subject with him today."

"You're kidding."

He chuckled again. "As distasteful as it sometimes is, this is what I do for a living, Mark."

"I thought you just edited bird columns and stories

about the Santa Claus Parade."

"That, too. Anyway, I guess you're not coming."

"As much as I'd love to, ha ha, I can't anyway. Buried in work today."

He sighed. Not a Rosemary sigh, but getting there. "I'll call Dorothy and see if she can go with me. Then I'll hire her after we go back to the office. We haven't had our meeting yet."

"Sounds like a plan, Stan."

"I'll let you know how it goes."

"Thanks," I said, not really meaning it.

CHAPTER

Twenty-Six

The next morning was clear and bright. I was relieved, because I'd arranged for a roofing guy to come around and do some work. I'd noticed some of the tin was lifting up on the weather side of the house, and figured that the screws needed to be replaced. The last thing you want is for rain to be getting up underneath the sheets and working its destructive forces. Much more expensive a proposition to re-roof than to refasten.

I'd found someone through Kijiji who was advertising weekend odd jobs. When I'd called him up, several weeks ago, he said he worked for a local company, Blanchard Roofing, and had their blessing to moonlight on Saturdays for the extra income. He gave me a name and number, and I called the company to check him out. They said good things, so I called him back and made an appointment.

He showed up on time, not long after I'd finished breakfast. He ran up his extension ladder, took a look, and came down to tell me what he would need to do. A number of screws on this side of the roof were either lifting or broken, so he recommended refastening the entire surface. He said it would be a three-hour job, gave me a price I thought was fair, and gave me a business card when we shook hands on it.

"It's my company's card, but it's got my name and cell number in case you need to reach me."

"Thanks." I put it in my shirt pocket. "I'm going to grab some coffee. Would you like anything?"

"A cold beer if you've got one." He grinned. "Just kidding. I brought water with me."

I nodded and went inside as he got to work.

I put a load of laundry in the washing machine and went upstairs to my bedroom. At the back of the walk-in closet I had a small safe installed in the wall. I opened it and counted out the amount he'd mentioned, plus an additional twenty as thanks for having shown up as promised. It was sometimes difficult to get trades people to travel outside the town limits for small jobs, and I always appreciated it when they did.

I poured my coffee and took it out onto the back deck with Thursday's *Sentinel*. I hadn't had a chance to read Patrick's article on Nathan and, truth be told, I also wanted a second look at the illustration I'd sold him.

It still looked good. I settled down to read. I wasn't directly in the roofer's line of sight, so it wasn't as though I was keeping an eye on him. I could hear him working away, and that was good enough for me.

I thought Patrick had done a very good job with the article. Grace was presented in a very sympathetic light, and the pathos of the situation came through effectively without being overwhelming. He was an excellent writer. He certainly did have a very promising future ahead of him.

I put the paper aside and drank some coffee. The air

was pleasant and the breeze was slightly cool. I felt good because Adrienne had bought two of my gags last night, along with one of the covers I'd sent, and I'd been able to give her the finals in time for her to fit them into the issue. Playing beat the clock was, I had to admit, a bit of a rush. Pun intended.

I closed my eyes. The sun felt warm on my skin. I think I dozed off.

The roofer walked around the corner of the house. I opened my eyes as he came up the stairs onto the deck.

"Mind if I sit down for a minute?"

"Make yourself comfortable." I sat up straight and reached for my coffee.

"Ten-minute break," he said, opening a bottle of water and taking a drink.

"Sounds like a good idea. At least it's a nice day to be working outside."

"Yeah." He was a small, nondescript man in his late thirties or early forties. His dark hair arced across his forehead in a widow's peak, and his skin was tanned and leathery, no doubt a by-product of his trade.

His eyes went to the newspaper I'd left folded at Nathan's story. He drew it over with a finger, read the headline, and muttered "Shit."

He picked it up and began to read.

As he did, I realized I didn't remember his name. He'd told me on the phone, of course, but it had slipped my mind. If we were going to chat, I thought it would be polite to be able to speak to him by name.

I took his card out of my pocket.

John Forrest.

It took me a moment. *Oh, Christ.*

Peter Forrest's father.

I'd booked the appointment with him before all this with Rosemary and the missing persons had started, and I'd immediately forgotten his name after speaking to him.

I closed my eyes and resisted the impulse to get up and go into the house. What were the odds? I mean, really? I didn't believe in coincidences, but there he was, Peter Forrest's father, sitting across the table from me.

He finished reading the article and put the paper down. "I know exactly how that woman feels. My boy disappeared almost ten months ago."

"My God. That's terrible."

"It was like this young guy, Notwell." He looked at the newspaper. "One moment he's there, and the next he's gone. For good. Only with Pete, he went for a run and never came back."

"I'm very sorry."

"Thanks." He swallowed more water and wiped his mouth with the back of his hand. "His mom died when he was six. I've been trying to raise him on my own, but it's not easy. He was about to graduate and was trying to decide what to do next."

He picked up the water bottle, looked at it, and drank, "Plus, it didn't help that I've got a booze problem."

I didn't say anything. What could I say?

"I was drinking when Pete went out. I fell asleep on the couch. It was nearly midnight when I woke up and realized he wasn't there. I went out and looked all over the place. It's my fault. I let him down."

He stared off at the distant treeline. "Don't know why I'm telling you all this. You don't know me from Adam."

"It's all right," I said. "Talk is good."

"Yeah." He glanced at me. "I saw your name with the drawing of the Nathan guy. You're an artist, are you?"

"Yeah."

"Must make a good living at it. Nice place."

"Thanks."

"I take on the extra work to make ends meet, given how much stuff costs in the grocery store and at the gas pump, but the truth is I do it to stay busy. I can't stand being alone in that house. I quit drinking on Christmas Day and I haven't touched it since, but being alone in that house sometimes pushes me to the limit."

"What about the police? What do they say?"

"They did everything they could, I guess." He bit his lip. "Talked to his friends, teachers at school and his coaches, the whole nine yards. Nothing. It was like he just vanished into thin air."

I had to ask. I was in too deep with him right now not to. "Do you think there's a connection between your son's disappearance and Nathan Notwell?"

He took a long time to answer. "I don't know. I never heard of this guy before. I didn't know this had happened until just now. I generally don't read the paper."

"What school did Peter go to?"

"Saint Ignatius High. We're only a block away. I'm a lapsed Catholic. Another thing to feel guilty about. But I wanted him to go to a good school and it was in walking distance." He rubbed his forehead. "He was such a good kid. Very patient with me. Missed his mom a lot, but helped me out as much as he could. Good at sports; did I mention that? Played hockey in the winter for Saint Ignatius and baseball in the summer. The other kids liked him."

He put the cap on his bottle of water and stood up. "I've bored you enough with this. Time to get back to work. Can I use your washroom?"

"Sure," I said. "I'll show you where it is."

CHAPTER

Twenty-Seven

That evening, Patrick called me with an update.

I was in the solarium, reading *Labyrinths* by Jorge Luis Borges. I'd read it many years ago as a young buck searching for inspiration, and after learning that his widow had recently died intestate and a judge had ruled that the rights to all his work would pass down to his nephews, I was curious to revisit the collection and refresh my memory.

I was halfway through "The Zahir," which had always been my favourite Borges story, when the phone rang. It took me a moment to mark my place and pick up the portable.

"It's me."

"Patrick. How did it go?"

"Rough. He punched me in the mouth."

"What?" I was shocked.

"Right in front of Dorothy, sitting there as a witness."

"Are you all right?"

"Well, I've got a dentist appointment for a loose tooth. I think it'll have to come out. What do you know about implants?"

"They're expensive."

"Yeah. Anyway, I think the picture is clearer now on Sampson and his anger problems. After I got sitting down again with a wad of tissues on my mouth, I mentioned that a friend had tipped me off on it, and the criminal record that went along with it. His answer? He said, and I quote, 'I'll bet it's that fucking asshole Ferguson. Son of a bitch.' Apparently they'd had a falling out, and this other guy has been trying to smear him around town."

"I see. So where does that leave us, Patrick?"

"I don't really know. The friend had mentioned convictions for assault and forcible confinement, which rings all the bells, but I don't really get how that would extend to Nathan and the other two. He claims not to know them, and at the moment I really can't see a way to prove otherwise."

"What motive would he have for kidnapping his niece?"

"Yeah. That's the other thing. We don't know enough about him yet. Plus, you have to figure that Shepard has already gone down this road without finding something to bring him in on."

I hesitated. Ah well. In for a penny, in for a pound. "I have an update for you."

"Don't tell me Shepard came around again."

"No, thank God." I gave him a *Reader's Digest* version of my conversation with John Forrest.

"Wow," he said when I was done. "Talk about synchronicity."

"Yeah, I guess."

"Did he mention anything that might connect to the other disappearances?"

"No, not really."

He paused for a moment, thinking. "All right. I think I'll put Emily and Nathan on the back burner for now and dig around on Peter Forrest. Make a few calls."

"Are you sure you're up to it? You don't have any concussion symptoms, do you? Could Dorothy take over?"

"No, I'm fine. Nothing a little ibuprofen can't handle. A lot, actually. Anyway, I'll tell you one thing. It was a good job Rosemary wasn't there or she'd have clocked the guy right back. Then we would have had the cops down our necks again and the shit would have really hit the fan."

"You didn't call her?"

"I did, but she couldn't come. She was in a really foul mood, even for her. She said something about the township and strangling somebody and hung up on me."

"Sounds like she's got a problem."

"She has a few, so what's one more, right? Talk to you later."

We ended the call and I went back to "The Zahir," the story of an insignificant coin with the power to cause a person who sees it to become totally obsessed with it, until finally nothing else exists for them but the coin, and they lose all touch with reality.

Hmm.

CHAPTER

Twenty-Eight

My morning began with a call from Bob Champion. He and May were in Paris, which was six hours ahead of us slugs languishing back here in eastern daylight time, and they were enjoying a late lunch at some café on the Left Bank, the name of which I was supposed to recognize but didn't.

After exchanging pleasantries, he said, "Listen, the reason I'm calling is I'm sitting here with Perrin Olsen and Jason Burbidge. You remember Perry, of course."

"Yeah, sure." Olsen was a successful book publisher whose imprint Moonlight Crime boasted a list that included some of the most famous crime fiction authors in the United Kingdom, many of them young talents bursting with hot bestsellers and an ambition to reach the top of the charts and stay there. Not too long ago, I'd read in *Publishers Weekly* that he'd recently sold out to the Random Penguin for an insane amount of money.

"How's he doing?"

"Wonderful. He's here on a little vaca, same as us, and we bumped into each other in the Louvre. So we decided to grab some lunch and catch up on things."

"Say hi for me."

"Mark says hi."

"Hi, Mark," said a voice in the background.

"Hi Mark," echoed a second voice. That would be Jason, Perrin's partner and companion.

"Anyway, just wanted to give you a heads-up. We got talking about you, and he said how much he's always admired your work. He's started up another company, did you know that?"

"No, but it doesn't surprise me."

"Yeah. One of his new imprints is called Rocking Horse Publications. Have I got that right, Perry?"

"Rocking Horse Press," the first voice in the background corrected.

"Press," Bob repeated. "It's more a general interest thing than the crime fiction stuff. He says he wonders if you'd be interested in doing a new collection with him. Your recent stuff. I told him I thought you weren't under contract for anything else right now."

Olsen was well known as having the golden touch when it came to books and book publishing. He was popular with the media as a high-flying independent who turned start-ups into dynamos with author lists that were five-star all the way. If he was interested in my work, then I was definitely flattered. And no, I had no contractual obligations for future collections.

"Sure," I said. "Why wouldn't I be?"

"He's interested."

"Yay," said a chorus in the background.

"So look, he's going to have Meg Bantree call you in a week or two to get things started. How's that sound?"

"Great." I knew that Olsen suffered from acute

telephonophobia, also known as phone anxiety. There were no phones in his office, not even an intercom system connecting him to his executive assistant, and of course he didn't own a cellphone. He had three homes, one in London, another in New York, and a third in the Bahamas, and while they all were equipped with landlines, the ringers were muted and only a flashing light indicated an incoming call.

Which he never answered. He relied on Jason or his domestic staff to handle phone duties as well as any follow-up required on messages left in voicemail.

While this was a highly unusual arrangement for any business person, let alone one of the top indie publishers in the world, it had never held him back. Other people did the work while he made the big decisions. A recipe for success in Olsen World.

After ending the call, I went into the studio and started browsing through my files, making a list of the gags I thought would work well together in the collection. I had the special occasion ones, of course—Halloween, Christmas, Thanksgiving—and the usual, including several desert-island gags, an airplane passenger joke, and a new electric car cartoon featuring a man asking the salesman: "Does it come with Flintstone feet in case the battery dies before I reach a charging station?"

I went for my walk after lunch and spent the afternoon reading in the solarium again. I'd finished the Borges book and was now re-reading *The Horse's Mouth* by Joyce Cary, a marvellous novel published in 1944. It was told from the point of view of Gulley Jimson, a painter long past his prime and reduced to a level of poverty so profound he'd do pretty much anything for a few coins to buy a brush and a tube of colour to pursue his obsession—painting. It was amusing, inspiring, and sad, all at once.

Once again, it took me back to my ambitious youth, when I'd first realized where my life's path lay, and some of the personal sacrifices we all had to make in order to succeed in the art world. A reminder of the obsessions that went with the territory.

Once again, I was deep into the story when the phone rang.

Once again, it was Patrick.

"Doing anything this afternoon, Mark?"

"Just some reading. Why, what's up?"

"We thought we might drop around and see how you're doing."

"Who's 'we'?"

"Myself and Rosie."

Rosie? "Sure, come on out."

I had coffee ready and waiting when they rumbled into the driveway and clomped up the stairs to ring the doorbell.

Rosemary didn't move when I opened the door. "We want to know if you're in or out."

"Yes. Important things to discuss." I got them inside and through the living room into the solarium. I took their orders and brought Patrick a bottle of Heineken and a glass, Rosemary a can of Coke (no glass), and a cup of coffee for myself. I sat down.

"In or out?" Rosemary repeated.

Patrick poured his beer. "We did some follow-up on Peter Forrest this afternoon."

"By all means," I said, looking at him over the rim of my coffee cup, "tell me about it."

"You'd mentioned that Mr. Forrest talked about his son being a good athlete. I made some calls and found out he'd played Little League baseball since he was five, and played in both the high school and local fastball leagues last year as a seventeen-year-old. I got the names of the team and the fastball league coach, and found out they had a game today. So Rosie and I went to the park to talk to him."

I glanced at Rosemary. She was staring at me with an odd expression on her face. Not hostile. Something else. "So, how did that go?"

"Curt Duffy's his name. He liked Pete. That's what everyone called him. Said he was the best player on the team every summer. Outgoing and friendly. Tall and athletic. Got along well with the other kids. Popular with the other parents because he usually helped his team win their games."

"It doesn't make sense. Why abduct someone like that?"

"Yeah, I know."

I looked at Rosemary. "What did you think of him?"

"Duffy? He's all right. Comes off as a good guy. Good with the kids. Not smarmy or creepy. Works for the RCMP and commutes to Ottawa. How does that sound to you?"

"Like he's probably not our kidnapper."

She nodded. "We asked him about last summer, and he said it was busier at the park than the last few years, because all the COVID stuff was being lifted and people were happy to get out and do stuff. So Patrick asked if there were any problems with people hanging around or being overly friendly with the players."

"At first he couldn't remember," Patrick said. "Then he said a few parents got out of hand and had to be talked to. He says he takes his Mountie ID with him to flash when there are close encounters like that. Last summer there were more than usual. Then, as he talked, he remembered some young guy hanging around most of the games."

"Duffy said he remembered him," Rosemary said, "because he reminded him at first of one of his nephews. Mid-twenties, black hair, nondescript. Didn't say or do anything, just hung around and stared at the players."

"Peter Forrest in particular?"

She shrugged. "He didn't think so. After a while the guy stopped showing up. It was a non-thing, but Duffy remembered him when we asked because of the resemblance to his nephew."

"We talked to a few of the parents," Patrick said. "I took a bunch of notes, but nobody remembered anything useful. A year ago is a long time for something that doesn't affect other people directly. A couple of them didn't even know which player I was talking about."

"One woman thought she remembered an older guy hanging around," Rosemary said, "but she was really vague about it. Said her son is a bit introverted and got upset because he thought the goober was staring at him."

"She also remembered the one who looked like Duffy's nephew. I asked if she could give us a description," Patrick said. "I thought maybe we could ask you to draw a sketch, but Rosie's right. She was so vague, none of it would have helped."

"Would you have?" Rosemary asked me.

"Talked to the woman and tried to sketch a likeness?"

"Sure."

"I knew it."

Patrick stood up, leaned over, and handed her a twenty-dollar bill.

"Told you," she said, stuffing it into her pocket.

"I'm going to get myself another coffee," I said, standing up. "How about refills all around?"

CHAPTER

Twenty-Nine

Sunday was Patrick's day off, so he wasn't feeling any pressure to rush back to the office and crawl into the harness again. Rosemary also was free for the day, so we settled in for a visit.

"I heard," Patrick said, pouring his second beer into his glass, "that you've got another possible book deal in the works."

I was stunned. "What the hell, Patrick? I only heard about it myself this morning."

He laughed. "Blame Dad. He was talking to Meg Bantree. Her younger sister used to work for him, remember? Maybe you don't, unless you read *Publishers Weekly* cover to cover. Anyway, he mentioned that you were doing gags for me when he was bragging to her about the *Sentinel*, and she got all excited because she'd just been told she'd be working with you on a book."

"My lord. Did your father also tell you what I had for breakfast?"

"Toast and coffee."

I looked at him.

"You always have toast and coffee."

"I don't understand," Rosemary said. "You're writing a book? I thought you were an artist, not a writer."

"It's a collection of my cartoons. Not nearly as much work as writing a book from scratch."

"It'll be his fourth collection," Patrick said.

Rosemary raised her eyebrows. "I thought artists were supposed to be poor and starving. Not you, though, eh?"

"I've done all right, I guess."

"I suppose you had rich parents, like this one." She shot a look at Patrick.

I smiled, tasting my coffee. "Not at all. My parents owned a dry cleaning business in Cobourg."

"Really."

"Yep. I was an expert shirt presser and folder when I was eight."

"Child labour," Patrick joked.

"Family business." I sat back, thinking about my father.

Rosemary raised her eyebrows. "So, okay, spill it. What were they like? Your parents?"

"They were good. Dad was a character. Good sense of humour. We were right downtown, and he'd sit on a bench on the sidewalk out front, smoking a cigarette and talking to everyone who went by. Joking about the weather and you name it. They used to say he should run for mayor, but he'd just laugh and say he'd rather leave the screwing up to somebody else."

"What about your mom?'

"She worked hard. She looked after the finances and all the rest of the stuff that keeps a business going. When I think of her now, I picture her as always looking tired. But very positive. She was a very positive person. Happy. In a tired sort of way."

"Must be nice."

"To have had parents like that? Yeah. I was very lucky."

I kept thinking. "You know, things were so different back then. The beach was great, the sand was clean, and it was good swimming. My friends and I used to walk down on Sundays to hit the water when Mom and Dad had the day off. It was incredible. I'd stay the longest and usually ended up walking home by myself."

"Cobourg has a beach?"

"Damn right. Best beach on Lake Ontario by far. Clean sand, nice water, a boardwalk. I miss it." I shook my head. "Back then, young people could walk around town by themselves and not be afraid."

No one spoke for a while.

Patrick stirred. "We're at a disadvantage with Pete because it was a year ago, and memories fade. And we're not even sure exactly where he disappeared because he was jogging, and no one knows what his route was. He could have been grabbed anywhere along the way."

"I don't get that one," Rosemary said. "Young athlete like him. How would they overpower him and take him away somewhere?"

"Chloroform, maybe. I don't know." Patrick drained his glass and stood up. "We should let you get back to your reading, Mark." He looked at Rosemary. "Can I bum a ride home?"

She nodded. As she passed me, she reached out and touched my arm. "In or out?"

"In," I said. "I just don't know what else we can do at this point, that's all."

CHAPTER

Thirty

It was only mid-afternoon, and I was feeling restless after they left, so I decided to go for a drive. I put a fresh cigar in my travelling case, grabbed my keys, and headed into town.

I wanted to revisit the various places I'd been while looking for information about the disappearances. I wasn't really sure why, other than to refresh my memory and see if any new and useful ideas occurred to me. It was a quiet Sunday; traffic was light; and it was good driving weather after yesterday's storm.

Once in town I turned down Bridge Street and stopped at the river. The storm had thrown a lot of tree branches and other debris into the water, and I watched them bob and weave along the surface and out of sight under the tree cover. I realized I hadn't sketched this place, and thought about it for a moment. The last thing I wanted to do was run into Tom O'Toole again, but I saw that if I sat down on the edge of the sidewalk, I could see enough of the river, the bridge on an angle, and the shoreline that Nathan would have explored with his friend Renata and her companion dog, Butterscotch.

I got out, grabbed my art box and sketchbook, set up my little stool, and got to work.

A car passed behind me, crossing the bridge, and I looked over my shoulder, suddenly worried that it might be a police cruiser that would stop, its uniformed occupant wanting to know what the hell I was doing here. Shepard and company obviously had me spooked. Thoughts of arrest and interrogation bounced around in my head, but it was only someone in a dusty Volkswagen Jetta, and it was quickly gone.

I turned the page and began a new drawing, concentrating a bit farther downstream and including some of the tree cover. As I drew, I thought. Nathan was not likely to have been snatched here; it was fairly well determined by everyone involved that it had happened between the park and his home, but what if he'd made a detour down here for a little rock-skipping?

I finished the drawing and shifted my stool so I could see a little more of the side of the bridge. Did I think O'Toole was a viable suspect, when Shepard and his colleagues definitely did not? I couldn't see how he could be ruled out.

As I drew, I became conscious of a robin that was raising a ruckus around me. It kept flying from the trees to the railing of the bridge and back again, cheeping at the top of its lungs. It must have a nest nearby and was upset by my presence.

I didn't remember the noise from before, when Rosemary and I had confronted O'Toole. Perhaps I just hadn't paid attention.

Sound was a dimension that was missing from my sketches, wasn't it? Obviously—no-brainer, Mark—but did it mean something? Was I missing something connected to the sounds of nature or noise or something or other of an auditory nature that would help unravel the mystery?

Nothing came to mind.

I packed up and drove off. Next closest was the park where Patrick had found Peter Forrest's fastball coach. I'd never been here before, so I was interested to see what it looked like.

It was a typical small-town baseball field. Page wire fencing ran all the way down the first-base and third-base lines, with flagpoles at the ends flying our Canadian flag. Each side had a dugout that looked like a shelter at a bus stop, with a tin roof and cement block walls. The backstop was a large half-cage hanging well out over home plate to catch foul balls and errant throws from the field.

The baselines had been scuffed up from the action earlier today, but the bases had been left in place so that the kids I was looking at as I sat down in the first-base bleachers could play their own game, now that scheduled league games were done and everyone else had left.

There were no adults, just eight kids playing a game of scrub. There were three batters, including a kid dancing off second base, the kid at bat, and one in the hole, waiting her turn. That left five kids, one to pitch, one to catch, one to cover first, one to cover third and left field, and one to cover centre and right field.

They were having a great time, yelling at the pitcher and batter with equal vehemence. Oh, how well I remembered this game! I'd much preferred it to teams, which got cliquey and overly competitive. No one bothered to keep score in scrubs, because the entire objective was to avoid making an out while circling the bases and reaching home safely. When someone did make an out, they moved into left field and everyone moved up a spot. Since batting was much more fun than fielding, you tried to reach base and stay there until someone came up behind you who was good enough to drive you in, so you could bat again.

I could still picture my friends and how they played when we were out at recess. One, a tall and lanky boy named John Campbell, rocked back and forth when he swung but always made good contact. Another, Dave Rogers, my best friend at the time, swung and missed a lot but when he hit the ball, it usually rolled all the way down to the school for a home run.

Endless hours of fun.

I drew to my heart's content and no one bothered me. One kid, currently playing catcher, glanced up at me as he grabbed a bottle of water at the backstop, but he said nothing and forgot about me as soon as he put his glove back on and pounded it with his fist for play to resume.

Again, Peter Forrest had not been kidnapped here. At most, it was a place where he'd been stalked and targeted, perhaps by an old man sitting by himself staring at the kids or by a twenty-something who resembled Coach Duffy's nephew. As I sketched, I listened to the kids, the shouts and laughter, the moans and groans, the ping of the ball on the aluminum bat, and the scuffing and pounding of feet. Did the soundscape tell me anything? Since I'd always been so reliant on visual input, I didn't really know one way or the other, but I listened anyway as I drew. It was a thing in my head now. Where would it lead? Who knew?

My next stop would be the other park, the one in which Nathan Notwell spent time while walking home from work. On the way, though, I realized I could first drive past the clinic where we'd talked to Emily Clement's mother. There was no shortage of spaces in the parking lot, since the clinic was closed on Sundays, so I took a spot at the far side, set up my stool in front of the Escalade's grill, and began to draw.

Once more, this was not the place where Emily had disappeared. It wouldn't tell me anything directly related to her kidnapping—which I'd come to believe it was, and not a drowning as the official story had it. This place contained no visual clues. But I wanted to draw it anyway. And again, I listened as I drew. I heard soft traffic noises, the pinging of the metal lanyard on the flagpole, crows in the distance. Nothing significant.

I sketched in the white vans that were parked by the side entrance. Two had the logo of Butler Brothers Janitorial Services on the side, while the third, also white, was unmarked and in decidedly worse condition than the other two.

They were probably continuing the cleanup from the broken water pipe. I thought of the young man who'd walked in on us while we were talking. What was his name again? It was a memory test, which I passed: Martin.

I packed up and continued on to the park where Nathan Notwell had last been seen. I chose a different bench this time, on the other side of the park near the side street. It gave me a completely different perspective, so I jumped right in, sketching the bench where I'd sat last time, the dry fountain, and other things I hadn't seen before.

I was well into my fourth sketch, eyes down, when a voice spoke behind me.

"Hello. You're an artist."

I nearly jumped out of my skin. Have I mentioned before I'm glad I have a healthy heart?

She came around the side of the bench to smile at me. I recognized her as the woman with the Airedale that I'd included in my sketches last Saturday. She had the dog with her on a thick leather leash.

"Hello." I looked down at the dog, which was sniffing the cuffs of my trousers. It glanced up at me with friendly eyes and continued to sniff, tail moving back and forth.

"No, Buzzy." She tugged on the leash, pulling the dog away.

"It's all right, I don't mind. I like dogs."

"He's overly friendly sometimes, but he's a good dog. Great company."

I looked at her left hand, didn't see a ring, then noticed that all the gear had been moved to her right hand. "Lovely day today."

"Yes, it is. I saw you last weekend, didn't I, on that bench over there?"

"Yes, you probably did."

"Have you just moved into the neighbourhood?"

"No, I live out of town. In Drummond Township."

She nodded. "Do you mind if I sit down for a moment?"

I scooted over to make room.

She settled down and pulled the dog close. He sat beside her.

"He's well behaved," I said.

"Yes, he is. Where in Drummond, if you don't mind my asking?"

"Tennyson Road."

"'To strive, to seek, to find, and not to yield,'" she said. "My favourite poem by my favourite poet."

"'And this gray spirit yearning in desire, to follow knowledge like a sinking star beyond the utmost bound of human thought."

She held out her hand. "I'm Darlene Leahy."

"Mark Heron." Her grip was firm and cool.

"Buzzy and I walk through this park twice a day, every day, winter and summer. It used to be nicer than this. They planted beautiful tulips and there were colourful perennials. But not any more. Budget cuts, they say. I wonder if Tennyson wrote a poem about the perfidy of civil servants."

I smiled. "Perhaps not, since he would have qualified as one."

"As poet laureate. You're right about that."

"What about you, Darlene? Do you live in the neighbourhood?"

"Down at the end of the block." She nodded at Maple Street, behind us. In a big, empty three-storey brick house with all my late husband's family heirlooms in too many rooms, and only an old dog to help fill up the empty space. But I'm whining. Forget I said anything at all."

"This seems like a nice part of town."

She waved her hand behind my back. "Gentry on this side. Third- and fourth-generation townies with family money and quiet lifestyles. And over here on the other side of the street," she waved her hand over the dog's head, who looked up to watch it move back and forth, "the proletariat. The same street, running from the school right down to the south end of town, but very different worlds depending on which side you're on."

I closed my sketchbook. "A young man disappeared from this park in June."

"I had no idea until I read about it in the paper. Terrible thing."

"Yes, and it's so quiet around here."

"Usually it is."

"Sometimes it's not?"

She made a face. "There are a few people who think it's entertaining to roar up and down the street after dark in the noisiest vehicles you ever heard in your life."

"That's too bad. Going through a stage, I guess."

"I suppose so."

"Have you seen them, or just heard them?"

"Oh, I've seen them. Hopped-up muscle cars with big tires and double exhaust. They like to lay rubber and drag race each other down the street. You can see the marks on the pavement."

"Sounds dangerous."

She nodded. "Very. Although sometimes it's just cars that badly need fixing."

"Oh?"

"A few times I've seen an old pickup truck or van or SUV or whatever it is going back and forth. I think his muffler must have a big hole in it, judging by the racket."

"What colour is it?"

"I don't know. Grey or silver, I guess."

I took out my wallet and handed her a business card. "I'm helping Nathan Notwell's family find out what happened to him. Not that the police aren't working on it. But we're trying to look at it from different angles. If you remember something, any kind of unusual activity around here in June, give me call. We'd appreciate any help we could get."

She turned the card over, found it blank, and turned it back. "Is this your cellphone number?"

"No, my landline. I have voicemail, so if I'm not there, just leave a message."

"All right." She stood up, and the dog stood up with

her. "I'll certainly call. And I hope I won't have to leave a message. I'd much rather talk to you person to person."

She tugged on the leash. "Come on, Buzzy. Let's finish our pee pees and go home."

I watched her walk away, curious to see if she'd look back. The dog led her to a tree, where he stopped and cocked his leg.

She looked back at me and smiled.

As our old cartoon friend Charlie Brown would say, "Good grief!"

CHAPTER

Thirty-One

On Monday morning I drove into town to buy a new electric can opener. Personally, I think all manufacturers of these infernal devices are secretly owned by Bart Simpson and are under strict orders to make products that foul up randomly, work a little while longer, and then become totally, completely, and infuriatingly useless.

I browsed in the bookstore downtown for a while and was astonished to find a used copy of *Saturday Slow* by Rowland Emett, also known as Emett of Punch. In my youth, Emett's intricate, eccentric cartoons had been among my very favourites. They were like Rube Goldbergs, causing your eye to travel up and down and over and under as you took in the strange landscapes and oddball characters in his gags. I opened the book and was further pleased to see that it was a 1948 first edition published by Faber and Faber and—low and behold!—it was signed by the author. What incredible luck!

Back out on the sidewalk, clutching my treasure, I decided to pay a visit to Patrick, since his office was upstairs. Inside, I found him hard at work, a woman I'd never seen before looking over his elbow at the screen from the chair beside him.

"Mark, hey. Pull up a seat. This is the world-famous Dorothy Kerr. Dorothy, meet Mark Heron."

We shook hands and I found a chair where I could see them both in profile. Dorothy was birdlike and middle-aged, her reddish-grey hair cut in a pageboy. Her small, dark eyes looked me up and down before zipping back to the monitor, watching as Patrick typed.

I realized he was a touch typist, a dying breed in this day and age. His fingers flew over the keyboard, and his right thumb pounded the spacebar after each word. He stopped and pointed at the screen.

"Is that better?"

"Yes." Dorothy stood up. "Save it and I'll finish up."

Patrick flicked keys with a flourish. "There. Thanks."

Dorothy Kerr gave me a friendly nod and walked out.

"We're working up a story to run in Thursday's edition that suggests a connection among the four disappearances."

I raised an eyebrow. "Isn't it a little early for that? We haven't really found anything concrete to connect them yet."

"I'm hoping the story will generate calls to Crime Stoppers and maybe new information will come out of it."

"What about Shepard? Have you talked to him about it yet?"

"I gave him a call this morning and told him what we were going to do."

"What'd he say?"

Patrick snorted. "First he tried the heavy-handed approach. That we'd cause a panic in the community for nothing, that we were blowing smoke and trying to sell copies, yadda yadda. I had to remind him we're a freebie. Then he said his response was 'no comment' and if I wanted anything else I'd have to call their media relations officer, Kim Malloy. So I called her next, explained the situation, and said that I could give her until one minute before midnight tomorrow night. Her last-chance deadline to provide a statement. We know each other and get along, so she took it calmly."

"Do you think you'll hear back from her?"

"God only knows."

I paused for a minute. "I drove around for a bit yesterday afternoon, revisiting all the spots we've been at while this thing's been going on."

Patrick said nothing, adjusting his glasses as he listened.

"One thing that occurred to me is that I haven't really been paying any attention to the soundscapes of these places. Once I thought about it I realized sound—noise, specifically—has come up a couple of times."

I told him about my conversation with Darlene Leahy and her Airedale, Buzzy, emphasizing her complaints about periodic traffic noise. "I wonder if it's important. Did it come up in any of your interviews?"

Patrick shook his head. Then he frowned and began rooting around on his desk. He pulled out a notebook and started thumbing through it.

"Yeah, here it is. Good job I learned shorthand so I can take notes and listen at the same time."

"Not to mention touch typing."

"Grade Nine was my best year in school, without a doubt. Here. I didn't assign it any importance at the time, just made a note of it along with all the other stuff people were saying."

He took a minute to read his pothooks and squiggles. "Yeah. When Rosie and I were at the ballpark. Remember the woman who thought she saw an old man and the young guy staring at the kids, but couldn't give us a description?"

"Yeah, sure. The guy who looked something like the coach's nephew, and the older fellow who just sat in the stands and creeped everyone out."

"That's it." Patrick tapped his notebook. "The woman said the older guy drove off in an unusual car of some kind. With a noisy engine."

"Did they seem to be together? The nephew look-alike and the old guy?"

"That's not the sense I got. Not at all."

I leaned back and closed my eyes, thinking it through. "Fine. It's a very, very slender thread, but maybe we should follow it. Remember Emily Clement?"

"Yeah."

"The old fool across the road complained about noisy traffic on the day she disappeared. He changed his story later on, but what if he'd actually been bothered by something and then got confused about it later because of the drinking?"

Patrick stared at me. "Jeez, Mark. It could possibly connect three of the disappearances. Noisy vehicles around the park where Nathan disappeared, a noisy car at the baseball park where Pete Forrest played, and a noisy vehicle of some kind the day Emily vanished. We haven't had a chance to look closely at Lucy Banner yet. What if it comes up with her, too?"

"Then we're looking at a predator with a loud vehicle." I shook my head. "Sounds kind of lame, doesn't it?"

"It's just about all we've got right now." He flipped the

corners of his notebook, making a buzzing sound. "We need to track down the older guy. With the noisy car. See if there's a direct connection between him and Pete Forrest."

"How on earth are we going to do that?"

Patrick pursed his lips. "Dunno. But I'll figure it out."

CHAPTER

Thirty-Two

Late in the afternoon he called me at home, and I could hear the excitement in his voice as he told me his story.

"I gave the problem to Dorothy. She's a bulldog with stuff like this. I don't think I mentioned before that she's from around here, although she was born in Halifax. Her family's from Drummond. The point is, she knows everybody and his dog. She worked for my predecessor for a long time, but they got into a fight and he fired her. A year or so before I bought the paper. Anyway, the point is, she's hardwired into this place. I got her to hit the phone, and she did her thing."

"What'd she find out?"

"First she called up the woman Rosie and I had talked to, who remembered the old guy driving off in a noisy car. She got a slightly better description of the car. A sports car of some kind, black with a lot of chrome trim. She also told Dorothy the old guy had a moustache and a tattoo of some kind on his forearm. Couldn't remember which arm. Jeez. So Dorothy started hitting the garages and dealerships to see if one of them recognized the description, if it resembled someone who brought their car in for servicing. If it's a sports car, the guy might be careful about looking after it, and the noise might be because it's a sports car and not a wreck."

"Sounds promising," I said. "Darlene Leahy said she'd seen that type of car in her neighbourhood."

"Yeah. So she finally struck gold. There's a guy on the edge of town who handles exotic and sports cars. He recognized the description right away and gave us a name. Lee Fogarty. Drives a 2010 Porsche 911 Carrera. Black with lots of chrome. Growly engine that makes a noise."

"Did she get an address?"

"The guy didn't feel comfortable giving out his customer's personal information, despite the fact he gave her his name and a description of his car. So Dorothy made some more calls and got it for us. Want to come with?"

I bit my lip. "You and Dorothy are interviewing him?"

"She's working on something else that has to make tonight's copy deadline."

"What about Rosemary?"

"She can't either. This thing with the township. Some kind of a meeting or something. Can you go with me? Bring your sketchbook?"

Ah, what the hell.

"Sure. What time will I pick you up?"

CHAPTER

Thirty-Three

Lee Fogarty lived in a very nice, nearly new house in a cul-de-sac on the western edge of town. The front lawn featured a red maple tree that was only a year or two from saplinghood, a lilac bush, and a small water fountain in a miniature pool with stone turtles and frogs around it. I pulled into the driveway in front of the two-car garage and parked next to the black Porsche Carrera.

"Looks like the place," Patrick said as we got out of the Escalade and walked up the cement path to the front porch.

"Guess he's home," I said, admiring the car.

The man who answered the door was not quite what I expected to see. Tall and lanky, he wore a blue and green Hawaiian shirt, blue jeans, and brown Birkenstocks. A cigarette stuck out of the corner of his mouth beneath his droopy white moustache. The watch on his right wrist was obviously a Rolex. His straight white hair was begging for a haircut.

"Yeah?"

"My name is Patrick Dillon, publisher of the *Sentinel*.

This is Mark Heron. Are you Mr. Lee Fogarty?"

"Yeah. *Sentinel*? What's this about?"

"May we come in and ask a few questions, Mr. Fogarty?"

"What about? I'm kinda busy at the moment."

"It'll only take a few moments. Please?"

He led us down the hallway to the living room. The furniture, nearly new, was upholstered in soft leather, and the half-empty bottle of beer on the coffee table was an expensive import.

He moved aside a laptop and sat down on the sofa. "Can I get you boys anything? Beer?"

"No, thank you, Mr. Fogarty. We won't stay long."

He closed the lid on his laptop and crossed his legs. "What can I do for you?"

"I'll get right to the point, sir. Several sources have told me you've been seen at the baseball park in town, watching the kids. I wonder if you could tell us why?"

I'd put on my reading glasses and taken out my sketchbook, the smaller one for less obtrusive work. As I drew his likeness in a few loose strokes, I picked up an odd vibe from him. There was something a little off, but I had no idea what. I was getting it in his eyes, which were sharp and critical, and in the set of his mouth.

Fogarty grunted. "Well, there's not much point in trying to hunt for big game around here, I'll agree with you. But a couple of kids have caught my eye."

I felt my blood run cold. Was he going to admit to us, right up front, that he was responsible for the disappearance of Peter Forrest and possibly others as well?

"They caught your eye." Patrick shifted uncomfortably. "What was it about them, exactly, that you liked so much?"

"Well, 'liked' isn't exactly the word I'd use. You can see potential, of course, which is what I'm there for, but they're still a little young. Just the same, if you can spot them at that age and follow them, who knows what'll happen, right?"

"Is that the way it worked with Nathan Notwell?"

"Notwell?" Fogarty shook his head. "Don't know him."

"What about Peter Forrest?"

Fogarty's eyes flared for a moment. "What do you know about him?"

"I know that he disappeared last summer, and that you were seen hanging around the park right around that time."

I was still watching Fogarty's eyes. They narrowed and then widened as he suddenly understood what Patrick was driving at.

"You're way off base, kid. Way off base." He raised the lid on his laptop and poked it back to life. "So you're saying he just vanished, is that it? I thought his family maybe just moved away somewhere."

Patrick shook his head. "That's kind of lame, don't you think?"

"Lame? What the hell's the matter with you? Don't you know who I am?"

"That's what we're trying to figure out."

"Well, let me help you a little with that. I take it you're not baseball fans." He included me in his glare. "In 1983 I set the National League record for saves with 24."

He turned over his left arm to show us a tattoo on the underside of his forearm. It consisted of the numbers "24" and "1983." I remembered one of Patrick's sources at the baseball park had mentioned that the old man she'd seen had had a tattoo on his arm.

"I pitched for the Cubs two more years after that, then signed with Seattle and finished it up out there."

"I don't understand," Patrick said. "What has this to do with a missing teenager?"

"Absolutely nothing, pal. That's my point."

"Then why were you hanging around the baseball park?"

Fogarty stared at us for a moment as though we were completely dense. "I'm a scout. You know, a baseball scout? I scout kids? Who play baseball?"

"You are?" Patrick looked at me. I grimaced, not knowing whether to believe him or not.

"Jesus, you guys. Did you just get off the spaceship from Mars, or what?" He raised his haunch and pulled out his wallet.

"Here." He handed Patrick a laminated card.

"'The *Richards Baseball Report*,'" Patrick read aloud. "It says Chicago, Illinois."

"That's right. We're one of the top independent scouting services going. My address is on the other side."

Patrick turned it over, looked at it, and passed it to me. I inspected it dubiously. Anyone could fudge up an ID card with Photoshop, a good printer, and a laminating machine.

I gave it back to Fogarty. He put it in his wallet, and I started a new sketch.

"Son," he said to Patrick, "let me set it out for you, so as to clear up any misconceptions you might have that none of us would want to see make it to print, because the lawyers are rich enough as it is without us contributing to their offshore retirement funds.

"Yeah, I'm a baseball scout. I started in after retiring from the Mariners, then got a job as an area scout for the Cubs. Calling in a few old favours, so to speak. After about a decade of that, Richards made me a phenomenal offer to work western Ontario for them, so I jumped at it. Three years ago they asked me to switch to eastern Ontario because they didn't have anybody here at all, so I said I'd do it for more money. Deal done. I cover from Belleville to Ottawa to Cornwall. Most of the time I'm on the road in the summer, but I've got a few days off right now, which is why you found me here."

"Are you saying," I put in, "that you were scouting Pete Forrest?"

Fogarty swirled his finger on the touchpad of his laptop, pressed a few keys, then turned it around so I could see it. "There's my note to file on him."

I leaned forward, squinting. Sure enough, it looked like a database for *Richards Baseball Report*, with a small photo of Peter and various fields populated with information including his age, measurements, and a text description.

"A kid like him," Fogarty said, "needs scouting reports on record that the universities and colleges in the good ole U.S. of A. can look at when they're deciding whether or not to offer him. I don't think Pete was good enough, but a decent scouting report from us would have helped his cause if he decided to walk on somewhere."

"Walk on?"

He rolled his eyes at me. "Jesus. Walk on. A kid who enrols without a scholarship but wants to try out for the team is called a walk-on. He signs up, walks into the dressing room, gets issued a uniform, and takes his shot."

"Do you think that's what Peter Forrest did? Walked on somewhere?"

Fogarty shrugged. "It's possible, but I doubt it." He tapped his laptop screen. "If he had, we would have heard about it, and we didn't. Division Three, juco, whatever. It'd be in here."

"Do you remember seeing a man in his mid-twenties sitting in the stands last summer? By himself, watching Peter while you were there?"

He shook his head. "You see families, mostly, or girlfriends. I'm talking about the summer fastball league, which is what you're talking about. At the high school games I talk to teachers and other students."

Looking at me, he asked, "You're drawing me, aren't you?"

"Yes, I am."

"Let's see."

I turned the sketchbook around and showed him, turning the page to show him the previous drawing as well.

"I'd like to have them, please."

I hesitated for a moment before thinking, *What the hell?* I signed both of them, tore them out of the book, and handed them over.

He looked at the signature. "Heron. If I Google you, will I find anything?"

"Might as well give it a try."

Patrick said, "Mr. Fogarty, I have to ask. Do you know anyone who lives on Maple Street or in that area of town?"

"Nope. Why?"

"Do you ever drive around in that neighbourhood?"

Setting aside the laptop and the drawings, Fogarty stood up. "No, and we're done here. Like I said, I got work to do. And if you print any crap about me, I'll sic my lawyers on you and sue you for every penny you got. *Capiche?*"

At the door, Patrick said, "Lawyers don't scare me, Mr.

Fogarty, and neither do lawsuits. People have gone missing, and they may already be dead. We don't know. We were hoping you might be able to help us, but apparently not."

"You were hoping I'd be your guy. Some psychopath watching teenagers play ball and then kidnapping them to enjoy a little deviant fun. Don't blow smoke at me, kid. You don't have the chutzpah for it."

"You wouldn't let us have a look around, would you? Maybe in your basement?"

"Get out before I throw you out, punk."

CHAPTER

Thirty-Four

That night I didn't sleep well again. I was starting to think I should buy a bottle of those melatonin gummies you see in the Walmart and try them out, in case they might help me get through the night with fewer wake-ups. Not to mention the trips to the washroom.

Around two, when I lay there trying to read myself back to sleep with the latest Michael Connelly novel, I began to think about Bill Lee. I wish I hadn't, because it cost me another two hours altogether.

Bill was from Brooklyn, a New Yorker through and through. He was sixteen years older than I was, and our paths never crossed, but I was a fervent admirer of his work. He had a loose, colourful style that was unmistakable. A familiar *Penthouse* contributor in the 1970s, he was a friend of publisher Bob Guccione and his wife Kathy Keeton. He also sold to their science magazine *Omni* and served as humour editor for both *Penthouse* and *Viva*, the latter being the couple's erotic magazine for women.

As the years passed, Bill seemed to drop out of the picture. His work became more scarce, and little was known about how and where he was spending his time. Friends such as Steven Heller, the *New York Times* Op-Ed art director, completely lost touch with him. It was an article published by Heller in his newsfeed a couple of years ago, however, that I couldn't stop thinking about.

As the story went, someone walking down the street passed a man on the sidewalk carrying an armful of pictures in frames. They soon reached a crew that was busily loading a bunch of them into the back of a garbage truck from a pile on the sidewalk in front of an apartment building. It appeared as though someone had died, and the contents of their apartment had been thrown out to make room for the next tenant.

The man stopped for a look. He picked up a large portfolio filled with artwork. Side by side with a couple of other pickers, he grabbed a set of binders of Kodachrome slides, many of them also artwork. He filled his arms, not knowing whose stuff it had been but sensing it might be important. The other two pickers did the same, while the balance was hauled to the dump along with rotting cabbages, dirty diapers, and discarded junk mail.

The man's wife e-mailed two friends, asking if they knew the artist responsible for the work salvaged by her husband, and while they did not, one of them forwarded the e-mail to Heller, who did indeed recognize it.

As Heller pointed out in his blog post, no one knew for sure if Bill Lee was dead and, if so, when he might have passed away. He was said to have had a daughter, but no family at all could be found, including his wife. It was as though everything to do with Bill had been wiped off the face of the earth. He would have been eighty-four when his stuff ended up on the sidewalk, so it was quite possible he was no longer around to keep it. Perhaps he'd been among the hundreds of elderly victims of COVID-19 in New York who were quickly and impersonally processed during that horrible crisis.

This story kept me awake (not for the first time) for a couple of reasons. First, Bill was an outstanding cartoonist, and his work was synonymous with 1970s satire and offbeat humour. Flip through any Guccione magazine during that period and you'd immediately know whose cartoon you were looking at without needing to check the signature. To say that he deserved a better end than this was a vast understatement.

Another reason had to do with the fact that all creative people, including cartoonists such as yours truly, soldier on through life in the hope that our work will outlast us, that it will carry forward well past our demise, preserving the essence of who we were as thinking, feeling, mortal human beings. A form of immortality in a universe where an actual afterlife is doubtful at best. Our voice, continuing to be heard, long after our pencil has been stilled.

Without the efforts of a few excited scavengers, Bill's entire legacy would have been tossed into a modern version of Sheol, the pit on the edge of the city where the bodies of the dead were cremated. A creative life dispatched to oblivion.

Memento mori.

The studio downstairs contained the collected works of Mark Heron, the original artwork that had formed the basis of a long and successful career, along with book proofs, signed copies of collections, original drawings by my favourite colleagues, and other valuable things. What would happen to it all after I was gone?

Once again I silently upbraided myself for not having prepared a will. The problem was, I had no family to pass all this stuff down to. I had friends, but many of them were like Bob, who was notoriously anti-materialistic and lived in a condo famous for its lack of objects. Minimalists who wouldn't want to be burdened with a lot of physical junk.

Yes, yes. Unlike myself. Mea culpa.

I suppose I could give specific items to specific people and then have the house and contents auctioned off, with the proceeds going to a charity. But there would be a lot of work involved in deciding who would get what, which auctioneer should be used, which charity, et cetera, et cetera. I kept telling myself I had better things to do with my time.

But the Big Seven-Oh was knocking. Death was hovering nearby, inviting me to join him in a game of chess.

Oh, God. Why couldn't somebody else do all this for me, so I could just carry on being busily humorous, or a reasonable facsimile of same?

I put the Connelly book aside and turned out the light. Staring at the ceiling, I reminded myself that four people— four among how many thousands—had never been allowed to have a full and complete life. Instead, they'd been turned into ghosts, whisked off the face of the earth.

I'd been fortunate. I'd made it farther than any of them. And I'd have a chance to see it all the way through, hopefully.

Somehow, the thought didn't exactly comfort me.

CHAPTER

Thirty-Five

The following morning, which was Tuesday, Rosemary and I met downtown in the parking lot across the street from Patrick's office. She gave my arm a little squeeze without explaining why, and we trotted through traffic and trudged up the stairs to the offices of the *Sentinel*.

We found Patrick with his feet up on the corner of his desk, a calico cat in his lap. He was sipping a cup of coffee and staring at the tin ceiling.

"It's copy editing day," he said, gently lowering the cat to the floor and sitting up as we dropped into chairs and got settled. "Everything's with Jane right now, and she'll take most of the day to work her magic."

"Jane Who?" Rosemary asked.

"Stewart. She's my copy editor. She'll flip everything back to me late this afternoon so we can make our midnight deadline for the layout."

"You wanted to see us?" I asked.

"Yeah." He grinned at me. "First of all, I think I'm getting to know you fairly well. I see you brought a portfolio case with you. Something for me?"

I unzipped the case and put an India ink and watercolour illustration on his desk. Well, on top of all the stuff on his desk. He looked at it, and the grin widened.

"Knew it. And from memory. We're in the presence of genius, Rosie."

It was a portrait of Lee Fogarty that I'd done last evening in the studio. "I want your word you won't run it with this next story."

"You have my word," he said, dropping the grin, "that I won't use it unless it's with a story about Fogarty's arrest." He glanced at his monitor. "I've put the next story about the missing persons on hold for a week."

"Oh?"

"I don't have enough. And I haven't looked closely at Lucy Banner yet, either."

"What about the OPP media relations person?" I asked. "Didn't you use the story as leverage to try to get a statement from her?"

He shrugged. "The deadline passed, and Kim didn't call. I'll let it ride for now."

"So where are you going to start with Lucy?"

"I went through our coverage of her disappearance in March. No witnesses, and as far as the OPP are concerned, they can't even tell exactly when she went missing on that day."

Rosemary stirred. "What day of the week was it?"

"Uh," Patrick lifted the corner of my artwork and pulled out a notebook. He flipped pages and said, "A Friday."

"She taught piano lessons? Out of her own place?"

"Yeah."

"Most music lessons are on Saturdays," I said.

Rosemary looked at me. "I've heard they're expensive."

"She was widowed at forty-six," Patrick said. "There was a large insurance settlement, so she was well off without the extra income."

"I suppose," I said, "the police have taken that into consideration as a possible motive for foul play."

Patrick shrugged. "It's a theory, although I think they like the one where she took off for a concert somewhere without telling anyone."

"Why? Why would she be kidnapped, if not for her money? Why, why, why?"

"Exactly," Patrick said.

Rosemary stirred. "The others didn't have money. Nathan and Gracie, zip. Same with the Forrests."

"Emily Clement was a librarian. Not exactly a high-paying job. And no support from her husband out west with his boyfriend because they never divorced."

Patrick was staring at his computer monitor. "Just a minute. I'm looking at Larry's follow-up article now. The sister-in-law, Allison Banner, said she dropped in to see Lucy that Saturday for supper, and she wasn't there."

"Neighbours? Anyone see anything?"

"They told Larry that there were no witnesses."

"Is the back yard fenced in?" I asked.

"Dunno. Let's take a look." He clicked, typed and clicked. "Google Maps," he said to Rosemary, who shrugged. "Here it is. Let me zoom in. No. Brother. There's a vacant lot behind it, on Coral Street. Someone could have walked right through and taken her out the back yard without being seen."

"We're getting exactly nowhere," she complained.

"That's one of the reasons I called you guys in for a team meeting this morning. I'm going to call a friend of mine, and I want you to be here."

"What friend?" Rosemary asked.

"Pam Corley. She's a missing persons blogger."

"You're kidding, right?"

"Not at all." Patrick folded his arms. "She's one of the top true crime bloggers in North America, not only in terms of views but also sponsorship money. She started out as an amateur, like the late Michelle McNamara, whose blog ten years ago was instrumental in the search for the Original Night Stalker, also known as the Golden State Killer. Who ended up being arrested after her death."

"I've heard of her," I said.

"Pam's focus on missing persons in Ontario has attracted a lot of attention. She's got an army of volunteer investigators out there working all hours on these cases, and whatever they find she posts on the blog. She calls it *Missing Until Found*."

"Catchy," I said.

Patrick nodded. "You've heard of Bellingcat? The people who do the open-source, ethical digital investigations of Russian military activities, illegal wildlife trade, and other stuff like that?"

"You know, I actually have."

"Well, she's built the same kind of independent investigation collective. It's really quite remarkable. I should have thought of her before."

He hit the speaker button on his landline phone and punched in a number.

We listened to it ring.

"*Missing Until Found*, Pamela Corley speaking. How may I help you?"

"Pam, hey. It's Patrick Dillon."

"Patrick! Great to hear your voice! It's been ages."

"Funny, Pam. It's been about three weeks. How did

Jack's root canal go?"

"Traumatic, as predicted. He's still whining about it."

"Ow. Look, I'm sitting with Mr. Mark Heron and Ms. Rosemary Nolan, sources who are working with me on a story. Do you have time for an exchange of information?"

"On the record or off?"

"A mix of both. I'll let you know when we're on."

"What's it about?"

Patrick glanced at his notebook and recited Lucy's date of birth, address, and basic description. "Can you find her in your registry?"

We listened to typing and clicking. "Yes. What about her?"

"Your last update was, uh," he glanced at his monitor, "April 28. That was the Monday after we ran a follow-up story. Should I assume you haven't gotten any further information on her since then?"

"Our investigators haven't found anything new. If they had, Patrick, we would have posted it."

"Understood. Off the record, for the benefit of Mark and Rosemary, could you explain a little bit how it works?"

"Sure. We're an investigative collective, so we have a whole roster of volunteers. Some of them are former police detectives still feeling connected to cases and wanting to stay involved, but the majority are true crime enthusiasts who follow up on leads and do a lot of documentary research for us. They don't get out and do field work, at least I ask them not to, because it's potentially dangerous and it might interfere with police activities, but you know what people are like. Sometimes they watch places, take a lot of notes and photographs, and send them in to me for analysis.

"Basic surveillance work," I said.

"Yes. Is that Mr. Heron?"

"Mark Heron, yes. Mark. In the case of Lucy Banner, do you have any way of checking into whether or not she travelled out of the country? Apparently the police here believe she took a trip to attend a music concert somewhere, which I guess she's done before."

"I was aware of that theory. We do, yes, have investigators who can look into that sort of thing. I won't go into details, but suffice it to say that we did a thorough check of every possible event across the globe that she might have attended, with negative results. In fact, we couldn't even confirm that she'd left the country."

"Sounds pretty comprehensive," I said, somewhat skeptically.

"Once you've built up a network like mine, Mark, you'd be amazed at what can be accomplished. Bellingcat was my model, and they've absolutely stunned the world by what they've been able to discover and publish. I hope to pull off something at least a little bit like that for all the missing people out there who need to be found and returned to their loved ones."

Patrick cleared his throat. "Pam, I'm working on a story that's looking into the disappearances of four people in this immediate area over the past year. We've spoken to the OPP about the possibility that they're connected, but we don't seem to be making any headway on that front."

"Four, did you say? Four?"

"Including Mrs. Banner." Patrick gave her the other names and their basic information. "We've been looking for threads that link them together, and granted it's been a difficult process but we've noted a few commonalities."

"Such as?"

"A noisy vehicle in the vicinity of each disappearance.

Three individuals—Nathan Notwell, Lucy Banner, and Peter Forrest—who lived within a few blocks of each other. I admit our information is sadly incomplete and circumstantial at this point, but the more we look, the more we find."

There was silence on the line for a moment. We could hear her keyboarding something. When she stopped, she said, "And you've passed this information on to the OPP?"

"Some of it. The rest has come to light since I last spoke to them. We've been met with indifference across the board on it, Pam."

"Hmm. Quite often police detectives prefer not to let on what they're thinking, Patrick. Who's the lead detective again?"

"Detective Constable Ron Shepard."

"Oh, yes. Here it is. I tell you what. I'm going to ask one of our volunteer investigators in your area to review the four cases, and then I'll give Detective Constable Shepard a call if I think we have something to share with him."

Patrick looked at me. I nodded.

He looked at Rosemary. She rolled her eyes.

"That would be much appreciated. The story's still in the research stage, so I can afford to wait. I'm just not sure how long these people can wait, though."

"Yes." She cleared her throat. "Now, before I let you go, there's something else I need to go over with you. All three of you."

CHAPTER

Thirty-Six

"This is on the record," she began, "so feel free to quote any part of what I say, or e-mail me for links to books and reports you should read."

"Fire away," Patrick said.

"Right now you're chasing down what could very well be a big story, and the adrenaline's flowing. Mr. Heron and Ms. Nolan, I expect you're on board with Patrick because you want to see justice done, and you want to rescue these people if it's still possible. That's all quite fine. Folks need to get involved when someone goes missing. We need an all-hands-on-deck mentality. That's why we have tip lines and eight-hundred numbers and a website with pages for each person. We *want* community involvement."

"Well, you certainly have it here in this room," Patrick said.

"Good. What I want to stress, though, is that you have to approach the families with particular care. Not that you haven't; Patrick, I know you well enough to know that you wouldn't behave in a way that would be counterproductive to the emotional well-being of these people. Mr. Heron and Ms. Nolan, I trust the same is true for the both of you as well."

"Of course," I said.

"When we're dealing with the families of missing persons, there's a psychological component you need to keep in mind. We can only imagine the hell that these people are suddenly plunged into. From the day their children are born, mothers and fathers feel a protectiveness that can be extremely strong in some cases. When a child disappears, the feelings of guilt, failure, and raw fear can be overwhelming. The same is true in the case of teenagers, like Peter Forrest. And you might think that the disappearance of an adult such as Nathan Notwell wouldn't have an impact, but he's clearly a dependent as far as his cousin is concerned, so the same psychological factors are in play."

"I have two boys," Pam said, "fine young men who are both at university. It's hard not having them in the house, because you worry, but I'm trusting they now have adequate life skills to look after themselves.

"When Rob was six, he disappeared in the Eaton Centre one day while he and I were out shopping. It was like I'd been struck by lightning. I had to go into the washroom to vomit. I could barely focus on what the security people were telling me. He was found after only half an hour, safe and sound, but at the time it felt like I'd been hit by a bus. I hope you don't think I'm over-dramatizing, because I'm not. It was one of the worst days of my life, and it only lasted a little less than thirty minutes."

"I think I understand," Patrick said.

"Imagine my state of mind if one of them went missing now. Do you think it would be any different? No. It would be exactly the same tidal wave of guilt, fear, and everything else. I wouldn't be able to sleep at night because someone I love isn't safe right now. I wouldn't eat, not only because my appetite would be gone but also because of the guilt. I'd feel like I don't deserve the luxury of food while my loved one is in danger. The police might give me an update and I'd feel a surge of hope because someone in authority is looking for them, but then nothing happens afterward and I crash all over again. I might sit in the same chair for hours on end, usually next to the phone, because I don't want to miss that call, whatever news it might bring, and besides, I wouldn't have the energy or interest to do anything physical like going for a walk or exercising or whatever."

I looked at Rosemary. She nodded, no doubt thinking of Grace.

"So people in this situation end up in a downward spiral of negative emotion that leads to physical consequences such as lack of proper nutrition, lack of proper sleep, and no exercise. Because of all that, the emotional crash is all that much worse.

"Time passes, and not everyone can recover psychologically. When a son or daughter is involved, no matter what the age, it can result in conflict between the parents. Separation, even divorce, sometimes follows. It's the same thing with a brother or sister, or a parent, or even a close friend.

"Those who make it through will go through stages. The emotional ups and downs, the flattened affect and sudden outbursts, all those things eventually resolve themselves, particularly if they're wise enough to seek professional help. They find a way to get busy again, either going back to work or picking up hobbies they'd set aside through guilt and mental inertia, or through other means. Some start a journal to write down their thoughts and feelings, working through them on paper.

"The fortunate ones, the strong ones, also manage to stay away from alcohol or drugs. Abuse is not uncommon in the early stages, but at some point they recognize the danger and pull themselves away from it.

"The most difficult hurdle of all is the self-blame. 'What should I have done differently? Where did I go wrong? Is it because I'm a bad person and don't deserve to have this individual in my life?' On top of that, their spouse and their children may blame them as well. That's where family counselling is essential. They need to remember that they love each other and they need to stay together for mutual support. So, if you're going to help in any way with these four families, please bear these factors in mind."

There was a moment's silence as we each digested what Pam had said. I glanced at Patrick, who was chewing his lip, and at Rosemary, whose eyes were on her hands. It was a sobering reminder of the reality being faced by Christine Clement, John Forrest, Allison Banner, and Grace Notwell. We all knew perfectly well we'd seen in them plain evidence of the trauma Pam had described so eloquently. We were each reviewing what we'd said and done in their presence. Had we been empathetic enough? Had we respected their situation and their struggles to deal with the enormous pressure they were under?

"Patrick," Pam said, "when you have a draft of your story finished may I take a look at it? Not to censor it, of course. But I may be able to suggest helpful amendments."

"Sure, Pam," he said from a long way away. "Thanks. Talk to you later."

"Talk to you later."

The call ended and we sat very still, lost in our own thoughts.

CHAPTER

Thirty-Seven

The next morning I was out on the front lawn, painting the wicker chair that I kept on the verandah for visitors, when I heard Rosemary pull into my driveway and rumble up behind the Escalade.

"Good morning, Rosemary," I said when she'd freed herself from her helmet.

"Hi." She ambled over. "Look, I can see I'm interrupting something real important, but do you have a minute to talk?"

"Sure." I put down the paintbrush and stripped off my latex gloves. "Give me a second to find you a chair."

"Don't bother." She followed me up the verandah stairs and sat down with her back against the railing post. It seemed to have become her favourite spot.

I dropped into the rocking chair and fired up a cigar stub. "What's up?"

She produced her cigarettes and took her time lighting up. It was a bit of a delaying tactic, I realized. Giving herself a moment to choose her words. I passed down the ashtray.

She put it next to her knee.

"I've got a problem. Maybe you could give me some advice."

"If I can."

"It's personal. Nothing to do with the people who are missing."

"Okay." Goodness only knew what she was going to come out with.

"You've seen my place."

"Yes."

"I gotta move. Soon."

I remembered Patrick having said something about her and the township. "Why?"

A long Rosemary sigh. "They're widening the road, because they're expanding the dump down there. They've moved back the road allowance, or whatever it's called, and my trailer's in the way. I gotta move it."

"That's too bad. Can't you just move it back, closer to your cousin's house?"

She shook her head. "Bryan's lot isn't zoned for trailer homes, and he never got a permit, which you're supposed to do. Basically I've been squatting, and because of this damned road work we've been nailed. He's going to get dinged pretty bad unless I move somewhere else. If I do, they said they wouldn't fine him."

"I'm sorry to hear that." I didn't know the first thing about municipal regulations or how zoning worked or anything that might be at all useful to her in this situation. But it was Rosemary, who'd definitely started to grow on me. "How can I help?"

She waved her cigarette. "I've been looking around. Checking out the trailer parks in the area. Their fees are just frigging astronomical. I mean, it's supposed to be affordable living, right? I don't know who the hell can pay what they're asking, man. It's ridiculous."

"I had no idea."

"So I've been making a lot of calls, trying to find a place by word of mouth. There's almost nothing available with a hydro hook-up, and the two guys I called who did have it wanted almost as much as the damned trailer parks. But I found a place on Kijiji that's actually pretty close to here. I was wondering if you'd come look at it with me."

"Sure. Where is it?"

She took out her cellphone and swiped at it. "On Webb. Know where that is?"

"Not exactly."

She turned her phone around and held it out to me. I put on my glasses and took it from her hand. Webb Side Road was a hop and a skip from here, indeed. A short little dogleg not far from Highway 7.

I gave her back the phone. "What time do you have to be there?"

She thumbed something to check the online clock. "In three-quarters of an hour."

"We've got a bit of time. Would you like a Coke?"

"No thanks. I'm good."

I drew on my cigar and blew the smoke out over the railing so that the breeze would carry it away from her. "How long have you been there? At Bryan's?"

"I roomed with him and Faith Ann for almost a year after I left home, but it was crowded and uncomfortable, so I started checking around for something of my own. Bryan knew a guy who was heading out west and was selling an Airstream, so he co-signed on a bank loan with me and I bought it. He said he could have just loaned me the money himself but he wanted me to start working on my own credit rating."

"Good idea," I said.

"One more payment next month and it's mine, free and clear. Damned bad timing."

I waited for her to continue.

She squinted at me through cigarette smoke. "You're dying to ask. 'Why'd you leave home, Rosemary?' So ask the question so you don't frigging explode."

"Why'd you leave home?"

She smiled without humour. "That's better, eh?"

"I don't want to intrude."

She made a rude noise and worked her cigarette some more. "Ancient history. My old man was a problem. Bricklayer who hadn't touched a brick in five years. Spent most of his welfare cheque on booze and weed. One night when I was sixteen he came after me, so I broke his nose for him. Knocked him out with one punch. That taught him to stay clear, but a few nights later my older brother tried the same thing. Broke his kneecap. Cleared out the next morning."

"Good lord. I'm sorry, Rosemary."

She gave me a look. "What the hell are you sorry for? I was already figuring out how to look after myself, so this just put a bow on it. The only real problem I have is making enough money right now to keep my head above water. The egg factory paid better than what I'm making now, but who can stand the stink? I guess I should go for my equivalency. Like May was talking about. Maybe I could find something better than a grocery store checkout clerk."

She stubbed out her cigarette. "Never mind that shit. Let's go look at this place."

I stood up. "I'll get my keys."

CHAPTER

Thirty-Eight

We followed the GPS on Rosemary's phone and quickly found a sign pointing down to Webb Side Road. As I slowed to make the turn, a newer-model grey car came out and went by us. The driver's eyes were down, but I immediately recognized Detective Constable Shepard. I swung around the corner with all due haste and kept one eye on the rear-view mirror to make sure he didn't double back and come after us. Rosemary had been looking at her phone, so she didn't notice.

After another minute or so her GPS announced that we'd reached our destination. The civic number on the little blue sign confirmed the fact. I turned into the driveway, trying to avoid the enormous potholes and ruts that threatened to disembowel the Escalade as we crept forward.

It was the kind of subsistence farm you see here and there around the countryside. A small pasture, maybe an acre in size, was cordoned off with electric fencing strung on metal rods. Inside were a few brown and white cows that I thought I recognized as Hereford, destined to end up in the back room freezer of the people who lived in the house we were heading toward. At the top of the lane, we rolled into a dooryard with the house on the right, a henhouse on the left, and in front of us a barn that had seen better days.

I pulled up close to the back door verandah where a woman stood with her arms folded, staring at us.

I got out and looked at a dilapidated old trailer. It had started out life with blue and white vinyl siding, but over time the blue had faded to light bile, and the white was now somewhere between cream and mud.

"Help you folks?"

Rosemary stepped forward. "Is this where Jerry Conway lives?"

The woman nodded. "What can I do for you?"

Behind the barn, the sound of children's voices reached us. Playing baseball or tag or something.

"I spoke to Mr. Conway on the phone. About his Kijiji ad."

Light dawned in her eyes. "Oh, okay. You must be talking about the trailer. It's right here."

She stepped down off the verandah to lead the way. She was short, and her choppy brown hair was held in place with bobby pins. She wore a horizontal-striped T-shirt, jeans, and black-and-red rubber boots. No watch, no jewelry, no makeup.

"There it is," she said, pointing. "When were you thinking of moving in?"

Rosemary stopped dead. "I don't understand."

"His mom just passed away, but I've cleaned it all out and it's ready for you when you want it."

"Can I talk to him? This isn't what he told me."

"He's in town." She folded her arms again. "What did he say?"

"We talked about me moving *my* trailer here. He said there was a hydro hook-up on its own meter, and the spot was all ready to go. We were going to negotiate the rent."

Mrs. Conway frowned. "There must be some confusion. He posted the ad to find a tenant for this trailer here, not for someone to bring another trailer in. We're not set up for another one."

"I'm sorry, that's what he said."

She shrugged. "I don't know; we didn't talk about it. He's been a little off since his mom died, so you'll have to forgive us if there was some kind of misunderstanding."

The children I'd heard a moment ago ran around the side of the barn and into the house, voices raised and arms flailing as they chased each other. I counted six altogether. They were a mismatched set—one girl was Black, three others had brownish-blond hair, and two boys were of east Indian persuasion.

Mrs. Conway looked over her shoulder at them, shaking her head. "What a pack of wild animals," she said. There was a smile on her face.

"Yours?" I asked.

"Foster. Jerry and I love having kids around. They all help with the chores, and I home school them."

"Have you brought any kids in recently, Mrs. Conway? Teenagers, maybe?"

"No. The most recent is Karim, nearly a year ago. He's nine. The children are usually here two or three years before they move on." She looked at me. "The detective who was just here asked me the same thing."

I pretended to be surprised. "Detective? A private detective?"

She shook her head. "OPP. Asked about a missing teen in town. I gave him the name and number of my contact at

Children's Aid. Maybe she can help."

I thought the first thing Shepard was likely to do when he made that call was check out Mrs. Conway herself.

During this conversation, Rosemary had been pacing back and forth. She stopped and blurted, "So there isn't a spot for rent here for my trailer?"

No, dear. I'm sorry."

Rosemary looked at me. "Let's roll."

CHAPTER

Thirty-Nine

I brought Rosemary back to the house and convinced her to stay for lunch. We ate in the solarium, watching a flock of crows horsing around in the field outside. We didn't say very much.

I made us BLTs, having some leftover bacon in the fridge from last night, and she devoured hers with a bottle of water. Her first sandwich went down angrily, but the intense flavours and carb hit did their work and the second one went down much more calmly. She accepted my offer of a cup of coffee, and after I cleared our dishes away and stacked them in the dishwasher, I sat down with her and picked up my phone.

"I'm going to call the real estate agent I bought this place through. Maybe she knows someone who can help."

I punched in the number from memory, after a brief moment's blankness. Retrieval from long-term, Mark. Important to be able to do. The call was answered after only two rings.

"Select Real Estate, Shirley Davis speaking."

"Shirley, hello, it's Mark Heron."

"Oh, hello Mr. Heron. How are you doing?" I could hear the reluctance in her voice. Unfortunately, I'd really put her through the hoops while looking for a property, and after a while I knew she'd come to dread seeing the Toronto area code on her call display.

"I'm well, thanks, and I hope you are too. Listen, I have you on speaker with a friend of mine, Rosemary Nolan. I was wondering if you might help us with a problem she has at the moment."

"What kind of problem, Mr. Heron?"

"Mark, please. Rosemary currently lives in an Airstream trailer on property owned by her cousin in Tay Valley township, but she's been ordered to move it and we're trying to find a spot for her to relocate. With a hydro hook-up and so on."

There was a long pause. "That's something I don't really deal with, Mark. Did you try the trailer parks? There are two of them in the area."

"Yes, she did, but they're far too expensive for her budget. Do you know of anyone, maybe someone whose place you sold recently, with that kind of set-up?"

"No, I'm sorry, I don't." Another long pause. "What you could do, though, is talk to the man who handles rentals here in the office. Bill Tunney. Would you like his number?"

"Sure, thanks." I looked at Rosemary, who had her cellphone out, presumably to the Contacts thing. When she nodded, I said, "Go ahead."

She repeated the name and recited the number. I thanked her, ended the call, and put the portable back in its charger.

"This is hopeless," Rosemary said.

"We won't give up." I bit my lip, thinking of how

she'd said that several times about the search for Nathan Notwell.

The portable rang. It was Patrick.

I answered, flipping it to speaker. "Patrick, how are you? I'm here with Rosemary."

"Hey Rosie," he said. "I'm glad I caught the both of you together. Would you like to come in and go over some things with me?"

"What about your paper? Isn't tomorrow your publication day?"

"Yeah, but I just put it to bed. Now it's in the hands of the printer, and I've got a few moments to breathe."

I looked at Rosemary.

"Sure," she said.

"We'll be there shortly," I said.

CHAPTER

Forty

We found Patrick out on the sidewalk, sitting on a bench in front of the bookstore. He was chatting to an older woman who was showing him the contents of her shopping bag.

"I really liked the TV show," she was saying, holding up a book, "but I've never read any of the novels, so I decided it was time."

"They're very good," Patrick said.

"The guy who plays Longmire is so polite and charming." She saw that Rosemary and I were waiting to speak to Patrick, so she dropped the book into the bag. "Nice talking to you."

He watched her walk away and stood up. "We can go upstairs or talk out here. It's a nice afternoon."

Rosemary sat down on the bench.

I looked around. There was very little foot traffic right now, and not much of a chance of being overheard if we were careful, so I sat down with her. After a moment's hesitation, I rumped over so that he could sit between us.

"I heard back from Pam," he said. "Her investigator got

right to work. He found out that Lucy Banner actually did have plans to leave the country after all. She booked a flight leaving for Vienna, Austria on March 22 but didn't board the plane. She reserved a room at the Hotel Beethoven Wien for a week but never checked in. She'd also paid for a ticket for a big Johann Strauss concert, but it went unclaimed at the box office."

"Impressive detective work," I said. "At least it confirms the OPP theory. The first part of it, anyway."

"She never made it as far as the airport," Rosemary grumbled.

Patrick waited for a pedestrian to pass before continuing. "He started looking at the other disappearances and told Pam about the same slender connections we've already found. She said he said he could see the smoke, and thought there was probably fire behind it. He's still looking."

"That takes a little pressure off," I said. "Our whole problem, Rosemary's and mine, is that we're amateurs, which means we're ghettoized by the police. Now at least these people are bringing some solid credibility to the table for us."

"Yeah. Pam also told me she called Detective Constable Shepard to share information she'd received on the Peter Forrest case. She gave him a thumbnail sketch of Lee Fogarty and his presence at Pete's baseball games. She said he took it in stride and promised to look into it. She pressed him on whether the other cases might be connected to Peter's, and he said he'd look into it further."

I told him about having seen Shepard on Webb Side Road, and I gave him a rundown on our visit to the Conway farm.

"Maybe it was on his to-do list," Patrick smiled. "Check out foster homes in the area, see if Peter was there or had passed through. Pam's call probably jiggled his elbow."

"He needs more than an elbow jiggle," Rosemary said.

"Yeah." He leaned toward her. "Are we still on for tomorrow?"

"Sure."

"Mark, could I ask a favour?"

"Of course, Patrick."

"Could you pick me up and take me out to Rosie's place tomorrow morning?"

"No problem. What's up?"

He smiled enigmatically. "You'll see."

CHAPTER

Forty-One

I picked up Patrick outside his apartment building, and as I drove south along Gore Street toward the far end of town, I could tell he was excited about something.

"So, what's up this morning?"

"Rosie's going to introduce me to her cousin."

"Bryan? Is that why you can hardly sit still?"

"Well, no."

"Then what?"

"You'll see."

It was obvious I wasn't going to get any more out of him, so I shut up and concentrated on my driving. And on a video call I'd had this morning with Meg Bantree, chief cook and bottle washer for Perrin Olsen at, what was it called again? Oh yes, Rocking Horse Press.

We chatted about the book proposal, a conversation that consisted mostly of her telling me which of my gags were her favourites. Once she came up for air, I mentioned a few I thought I'd like to include in the collection, and her response was casual and a little less bubbly. If I insisted, apparently, they could be worked in.

I smiled, thinking about it. Editors were all the same, weren't they? The book was theirs, the idea for it was theirs, the material was theirs, and any additional stuff proposed by the perpetrator of said material was to be handled with tact and diplomacy.

She e-mailed me the contract, which was in PDF file format. I signed it and saved it to my desktop before e-mailing it back to her. She wiped a tear from her cheek and ended the call.

The idea was to release the new book on the first Saturday of May next year. Her strategy, which no doubt had been approved by Perry Olsen beforehand, was to have it on the shelves that morning to coincide with Free Comic Book Day. Folks could drop into their favourite comic store, pick up their freebies, and buy a copy of Mark Heron's latest collection while they were there.

It was a plan, anyway. I had no idea whether comic book fans also bought cartoon collections, but the Olsen-Bantree team were superstars in the book publishing stratosphere whose ideas always worked, so if they liked it, I liked it.

The tear she'd wiped from her cheek needs an explanation.

Many moons ago, I was in London on a business trip. The big book fair was on, and I chatted with Perrin Olsen at their booth. He introduced me to Meg, who was working for him as an intern at the time. She was perhaps twenty-one or twenty-two, with a degree in her pocket and a head full of dreams after having found a spot inside the publishing industry.

Just a kid, really. About Rosemary's age.

That evening I stopped at a nearby pub for something to drink before dinner and found her at the bar, drunk as a skunk. Alarmed, I sat down beside her and extracted the story.

She'd answered a cellphone call from the head honcho of one of the biggest imprints—okay, Penguin—and, excited, tried to hand Olsen the phone. No one had briefed her, apparently, on his telephonophobia. He lost his temper and fired her on the spot.

The more she cried on my shoulder, the more frustrated I became, until finally I got her to her feet and said, "Come with me. We're going to get this straightened out right away."

"Oh, I can't. He told me he never wanted to see me again."

"He's a pissy little girl. Where is he right now?"

"We have a suite. Well, they do. In the hotel. For the imprint. For meetings."

I dragged her off. In the hotel elevator—all alone, thank goodness—she turned her head and threw up in the corner. We got off at the correct floor and I took her straight to the men's washroom. Ignoring the guy at the sinks who was washing his hands and trying not to grin, I got her cleaned up. I wiped off her dress with a towel, and I led her out.

Olsen was in a meeting in the bedroom. Someone told me he'd only be a few minutes longer, so I sat Meg down on a sofa and waited.

When he came out, I gave him enough time to shake hands with the guy, clap him on the shoulder, and see him out the door before I stepped in front of him and got right to it.

"This is not who you are," I said. "This is not the Perry Olsen I know. The Perry Olsen I know is empathetic, patient, kind. He wouldn't destroy a young woman's dream just as it was coming true."

"I'd rather not discuss it, Mark, if you don't mind."

"I do mind. What do you pay your interns, Perry?"

He made a face.

"Exactly," I said. "Meg Bantree's not here to get rich. She's not here working for free around the clock to take the kind of bullshit you handed her today. How the hell do you expect her to pay her rent and buy food to eat, for godsakes? Don't take her back as an intern. Hire her right now at the going rate and coach her up until she's the best acquiring editor you ever saw in your life. *That's* the Perry Olsen I know."

"No."

"Yes."

He closed his eyes. When he opened them again, he looked at Jason, who'd come into the room to listen. He looked at Meg. He looked at me.

"Ohhh, *shit*. All right."

Meg catapulted from the sofa and, instead of thanking Olsen, threw her arms around me and gave me a big hug.

We've been friends ever since.

The granddaughter I never had.

So, okay. Why bring this up now?

I was thinking about Meg as I eased into the parking lot in front of the bike garage on Otty Lake Side Road. Watching Rosemary saunter out of the open bay door to meet us, I felt as though I was making another friendship like the one I had with Meg.

It was just a feeling.

Patrick and I got out, and Rosemary led us inside.

"Bryan, this is Patrick Dillon," Rosemary said.

They shook hands.

"And this is Mark Heron."

I stepped forward and offered my hand. "You're Rosemary's cousin?"

"Yeah." His grip was vise-tight, but he let go quickly so as not to inflict serious injury.

He was a couple of inches shorter than I was, but the muscles beneath his black Harley T-shirt were major league—pectorals like steel breastplates; biceps that could crack walnuts; tattooed forearms as thick as my calves. His dark hair was trimmed short, and a thick white scar ran from the dimple in his chin to his right earlobe. His jaw was square and clean-shaven.

His hazel eyes held mine for a moment before he nodded. "You've been helping Rosie out. I appreciate that."

"Glad to."

Bryan rested his haunches on the edge of his World-War-Two-vintage metal desk and folded his arms. "So, Patrick. You're interested in a bike, are you?"

Oh ho, I thought. *Mystery solved.*

"Yeah, definitely." He shoved his hands into his pockets. "Is that it out front?"

"That's a bike, yeah."

"Jeez, Bryan," Rosemary burst out, "quit teasing him and get on with it."

He smiled at her. His eyes slid to Patrick. "Ever own a bike before?"

"No, sir."

"No licence."

"No, but I have a driver's licence. For a car. Although I don't have a car right now."

I pulled over a folding chair and sat down. I was surprised to see that Patrick was nervous. Excited, but nervous. Bryan Nolan clearly spooked him.

"It's a start. All right. So, the bike Rosie picked for you isn't a Harley. I hope that's not going to be a problem."

"I don't think so."

"Good. It's a damn fine bike. I'll tell you a little bit about it."

"Okay."

"In seventy-four, Nortons were a mixed bag. Some came out of the factory in great shape; others were shit. This one sat in a barn for thirty years on the farm of a buddy's parents in Prince Edward County, so it was a crapshoot. No telling if it was good or fucked up without buying it and working on it. I refurbished it from one end to the other. I replaced whatever parts needed new ones. Between what I paid for it and what I put into it, there's about seven grand in outlay altogether, not to mention my time. Which won't cost you anything, because bikes are not only my business but my hobby. How we doing so far?"

Patrick glanced at Rosemary. "Great."

"I'm not trying to snow you with stuff to confuse you. Rosie can talk to you later about it. The bike's a 1974 Norton Commando 850 roadster with the original gas tank and chrome. I rebuilt the engine and put new tires on it. In very good to excellent condition they sell for about ten to nineteen grand. I'm asking fourteen, and I don't like to barter. How we doing now?"

Patrick swallowed.

"Twelve," Rosemary said.

"Jesus, Rosie. What did I just say?"

"Twelve."

"Christ. I hate it when family gets involved in business. Nothing good ever comes out of it."

"Twelve."

"Shit. Piss. Damn. Thirteen."

"With a six-month warranty, parts only. Labour free."

"Are you kidding me?"

She stared at him, waiting.

"All right. Done."

She looked at Patrick. "Thirteen grand."

"Plus tax," Bryan said.

Rosemary stabbed him with a look.

"Okay, including tax."

"Let's go for a ride," Rosemary said to Patrick. "Then you can tell him yes or no."

Bryan tossed her the key.

We moved over to the front window and watched them go outside. They walked over to the bike, which was sitting underneath the big Harley-Davidson sign at the side of the road. It was a nice looking machine, all black and chrome with the Norton logo and model name in distinctive gold lettering.

Rosemary pointed out things on the bike and Patrick listened attentively, nodding his head. There were two helmets sitting on the seat. She handed him one and waited until he'd put it on and fastened the chin strap before donning her own. Then she mounted the bike and he slid into place behind her, wrapping his arms around her waist. She kicked the engine into life—only one kick necessary—and off they went.

"You know this guy?"

"For about two years now," I said. "Seems like a good kid. I know his parents. In Toronto. Good family."

Bryan grunted, staring out the window. "Better be. Rosie's getting interested in him."

I managed to contain my surprise. I suppose the indicators had been there for me to see, but I'd been stuck on her original pugnacity when we'd first gone up to visit him in his office twelve days ago. Apparently these things can happen fast.

I left the window and looked around the shop. It had

an open concept layout, with the office on one side and the garage on the other. From here I could see several bikes in various stages of disassembly on workbenches covered with parts and tools.

Here in the office, on shelves, was a collection of stuffed animals. The real kind. I looked at a deer head, a raccoon, a fish, and a raven. Taxidermy's not my thing, not by a long shot, but I said something polite about them to fill the silence.

"Yeah, I collect them." He left the window and wandered over to look at them with me. "There's more in the house. The deer I got while hunting. The pike I pulled from the lake just down the road. The raccoon I shot. Bastards get into my dumpster and make a hell of a mess. The raven was hit by a car right out front while I was sitting there having a smoke. I put some ice in a bucket and kept it cold until I could get it to my guy."

"Who does them for you?"

"Used to be an old geezer down toward Westport, name of McParland. Best in the area. All the stuff in the house is his. But he croaked and now I use this kid in town. He did all the ones you see in here. He's pretty damned good. McParland's widow recommended him, said he'd been the old man's apprentice for a couple of years."

We both turned at the sound of a motorcycle entering the parking lot. I could tell by the throaty rumble that it wasn't the Norton.

"Business," Bryan said. "Excuse me."

I went back to the window and stood on an angle to watch, hoping my nosiness wouldn't be obvious.

Bryan strolled out and shook hands with a young guy wearing a leather vest with gang colours on it. He took off a helmet designed to look like something that would have been worn by a World War Two German soldier. He started talking to Bryan and pointed at his bike. Then he broke off and stepped back as a second Harley rolled in. This guy was bigger, stockier, and about twenty years older. He parked and dismounted with his back to the shop, so that I could see the rocker panels on his vest: *Outlaws MC Ottawa*.

Bryan and the newcomer stood with their arms folded as the first guy went back to his explanation of what was wrong with his bike. Bryan knelt down and pointed, looking up, asking a question. The guy nodded, gesturing with his hands.

Bryan stood up and said something that made the guy frown. He said something else, about the length of a paragraph this time, and this time the guy nodded. They shook hands. The guy climbed up on the back of the second guy's bike, and they rumbled away.

Bryan wheeled the bike into his shop and closed the bay door.

I went outside through the office door and sat down on a bench against the wall. I took out a cigar and lit it. After a few moments, Bryan came out and sat down with me.

"Sun's behind the trees, or else it'd be too hot here," he said.

I drew on my cigar and nodded.

He took out his cigarettes and fired up one. "I retired six years ago, when Faith Ann and I got married. She wasn't in the life, and it was time for me to get out and start a family."

I glanced at him, saying nothing.

"It wasn't easy, but I was able to make a deal with them. From then on I was their go-to mechanic. For the whole damned lot of them. For the first five years it was free labour, just the cost of the parts. Which was fine by me, because I knew they'd hold up their end of it. Plus, I love working on bikes. Always have. On top of that, I'm damn good at it."

I nodded. I didn't think it was a subject I was qualified to say anything about.

"Bill's a good guy. The bike's his nephew's. The kid's kind of a dickhead, but what can you do. Most of them are assholes and you just deal with it. But some are like Bill. Friends of mine."

At that point the Norton reappeared on the road. We watched it decelerate and turn into the parking lot.

"Does Rosemary know?"

"About the guys? Yeah, sure. Why wouldn't she? They come in often enough. At least now they pay me for my work, so she stopped crabbing about it all the time."

Patrick slid off the bike and let out a rebel yell. Rosemary took off her helmet and shook her head, a bemused smile on her face.

I guess it was a sale.

CHAPTER

Forty-Two

I spent Friday in the studio working up some new material to offer the world, which was no doubt holding its breath in anticipation of my latest outburst of wit. In the morning, I went through my files of discarded and unsold gags to see if anything sparked. Most cartoonists refer to these files as their "morgue," but I prefer to call them my "files." Sounds less grim. At any rate, I pulled out a dozen or so and set them aside on the worktable to look at later.

The next step was to gather up my various sketchbooks to refresh my memory on what had caught my eye over the past year or so. Several drawings suggested gag ideas, so I got out the paper and started working.

By mid-afternoon my brain was fried, but I had a decent batch of possibles.

On Saturday morning, with a good night's sleep behind me, I discarded half of the pile, re-filing them where I'd found them, and I scribbled out a few new ideas that had occurred to me while I was browsing.

There were three in particular that I liked, and I was about to redraw them as roughs when the phone rang. It was Rosemary.

"Come pick me up, will you? There's somebody we need to talk to."

"Good morning, Rosemary. How are you today?"

"Yeah, yeah. What time can you be here?"

"Well, let's see. I'm working this morning. How about this afternoon?"

"Are you sure? You can't come now?"

"Is it urgent?"

A long, drawn-out Rosemary sigh. "No. I guess not. This afternoon. One?"

"I'll be there."

She was waiting for me on the corner across from the bike shop, wearing a black muscle shirt, jeans, and the usual cowboy boots. She slipped on a pair of sunglasses and stared straight ahead.

"So . . . who are we going to see?"

"His name's Safi. He lives on the same block as Lucy Banner. You remember where that is?"

"Yes, of course." I wasn't sure if I should be offended by her expression of doubt about my memory, but then, it was Rosemary. I'd already decided somewhere along the way that she'd have to work very, very hard to offend me.

We drove past the Notwell place and on to the next block. "It's one-oh-two," she said.

I looked at the street numbers on the tenements as we rolled past. Odd numbers on my right, even numbers across the street. I pulled up across from 102 and shut off the engine. At the moment, there was no other traffic. A teenaged girl passed along the sidewalk, walking a cat trucked out in a halter and leash. The cat was fluffy and orange, and the girl was Black. She waved at a boy sitting on the front steps of 102. He waved back.

I grabbed my small sketchbook and a grease pencil, and we got out. On the sidewalk in front of the tenement, I was about to ask the kid if he knew where we could find Safi when Rosemary sat down on the steps beside him and held out her hand.

"I'm Rosie. This is Mr. Heron. Jalil said you were okay to talk to us."

He shifted a little spiral notebook to his left hand and touched her fingers. He was small, dark-haired and dark-eyed, and he wore black-framed glasses that were a little too big for him.

"Yes. He said you were all right."

Rosemary looked at his notebook and pen. "What are you writing down?"

"Things."

"What kind of things?"

"Things I see on the street."

There was no room for me on the step, but there was a tree close at hand. I leaned up against it and began to sketch the two of them.

"What school do you go to, Safi?" Rosemary asked.

"Centennial."

"What grade are you in?"

"Five."

"How old are you?"

"Ten."

The screen door opened and a girl stepped out onto the porch. She wore a beige top, jeans, and sandals. Rosemary stood up.

Safi turned around. "Sulafa, Jalil said she's okay."

The girl looked at Rosemary. "What do you want?"

"We're looking for Lucy Banner. She lives across the street."

"The lady who disappeared."

"Yes. I've been asking around, and people say that Safi is the one I should talk to."

"Jalil said that?"

"Yeah."

I turned the page and started a sketch of Sulafa. I really wanted to know who Jalil was, but I knew better than to ask right now. It was my guess he was someone older in the neighbourhood who looked out for the welfare of the younger kids.

"Safi," Rosemary said, "they tell me you watch everything that happens in the street, and you write it down in your notebook."

He nodded, apparently not sure if Rosemary thought this was a good thing or a bad thing.

"Mrs. Banner was last seen on March 22. Did you write anything down in your notebook that day?"

"I'm pretty sure I would have. I write down things every day."

"Can you show me? What you wrote that day?"

He glanced at Sulafa. "It's in a different notebook."

"Could you get it for me? Would you mind?"

He looked at Sulafa again. She nodded. He got up and went inside.

The girl came over to the porch railing. "What are you doing?"

A sudden cold chill ran down my back. "Oh, dear. Are you Muslim?"

I couldn't believe how dense I'd been to start right in without asking first.

I'd learned about the principle known as aniconism, the

avoidance of images of living beings, while in Saudi Arabia. Although the Koran didn't explicitly forbid the practice of visual representation as such, sayings attributed to the prophet Mohammad threatened artists with punishment on Judgement Day should they produce images of human beings. Certain sects applied the concept differently than others. Without caring to explore the uneven landscape of modern Islam to any great degree, I learned at least to ask permission first before I drew a Muslim person's likeness. And here I was, carelessly scribbling away, oblivious to the offence I might be giving.

"We're Christian," she said. "I just want to know what you're doing."

Relief swept through me.

"He's an artist," Rosemary said. "He draws stuff. You're Safi's sister, right?"

"Can I see?" She leaned over the railing.

I turned the sketchbook around. I was finishing up a drawing that showed her in profile, looking at Rosemary.

She smiled. "Wow, that's cool. It looks like me."

"I'm glad you like it."

Her face turned serious. "We need to go in and talk to my mother."

Rosemary stood up. Sulafa led the way inside. I followed, holding the screen door. In the hallway I looked in at a small living room with almost no furniture. What was there—a couch, a recliner, a few folding chairs—were mismatched and obviously purchased at the local second-hand store. On the walls were a crucifix, several items of Eastern Orthodox iconography, and a large photograph, cracked and yellowed, of a man with white hair, dark eyebrows, and a dark moustache. Other photos were tucked into the corners of the frame.

In the kitchen, a woman turned away from the sink, wiping her hands with a dish towel.

"Mama, these people came to talk to Safi about his notebooks."

"Oh? Hello. My name is Malakia Nahas."

"I'm Mark Heron." I waited to see if she'd offer her hand, but she didn't, so I just smiled and nodded. "This is Rosemary Nolan."

"Please, sit down."

Rosemary and I took chairs at the kitchen table. It was a yellow Formica relic from the 1960s, with matching yellow upholstery on the chrome chairs.

"He's an artist," Sulafa said. "He drew my picture. You should see it, mama."

"I hope it was all right to draw her likeness," I said.

Malakia smiled. "It's fine."

I opened my notebook and showed her the first drawing of her I'd done in profile.

"My goodness, it does look just like you," she said to her daughter.

"You can have it, if you like." I glanced at Malakia. "If it's all right."

"That's very kind of you."

I signed it, tore it carefully from the sketchbook, and passed it over.

"Thank you so much!" The girl grinned, admiring it.

Rosemary and I accepted glasses of tea. I sipped mine; it was hot, sweet, and minty.

Rosemary asked, "You're from Syria, right?"

"Yes. From a Christian village in the mountains near the Lebanese border."

"I thought all Syrians were Muslims."

"At one point, in the 1960s, nearly a third of all Syrians

were Christian. Eastern Orthodox, mostly. Like ourselves. After war began in our country, it was reduced to 10 per cent. I don't know what it is now."

I set down my tea. "Do you know this other boy, Jalil?"

"Yes, he's the oldest child of the other family who came here with us. He's a teenager. A trustworthy young man."

At this point I noticed that Safi had slipped into the kitchen while we were talking. He took up a position behind his mother, a notebook in his hand.

"Your English is good," Rosemary said.

Malakia nodded. "Thank you. I was a teacher at our school in the village. Many of the books we used were in English."

"Mama speaks five languages," Sulafa said proudly. "Arabic, Greek, English, Turkish and Aramaic, which was the language spoken by Jesus."

"Papa's trying to learn English too," Safi piped up.

Malakia looked at me apologetically. "He wasn't born with a natural aptitude, as I was. It's hard for him."

"He's taking courses," Safi said.

"At the college," his mother confirmed. "English as a second language. If he ever hopes to get certified, he'll need it."

I frowned. "Certified?"

"At home, he was our doctor and the only surgeon for a hundred kilometers around. Here, he's not considered qualified. He must take courses and pass tests to receive certification, and, of course, to be able to communicate in English with his patients. So right now he stocks shelves at the hardware store and goes to his classes in the evenings to learn the language."

She looked behind her. "Safi, why don't you show them

what you have?"

The boy sat down on the chair beside Rosemary and opened the notebook.

"What was the date again?"

"March 22."

He flipped pages. It was the same kind of notebook he'd had outside, small, spiral-bound, with cardboard covers and lined pages. This one was well fingered and dog-eared, with several Post-it notes sticking out to mark entries he wanted to remember.

"Here it is. Oh, darn it. I remember now. I was sick."

"What?" Rosemary leaned over to look.

"I had a cold. I sat out too long the day before. It was cold, and it made me sick. See? I just wrote about having to stay in bed for the day." He flipped a few pages forward. "I could only do inside notes until Saturday, when I felt good enough to come back out again."

Rosemary gritted her teeth, restraining a curse.

"I'm sorry." He slowly returned to the page corresponding to March 22. "That's all there is." He idly turned back a page. "See, on the twenty-first I wrote down how cold it was outside."

Rosemary glanced at it, then frowned. "What's this?" She pointed at the facing page.

"The day before. Why? Oh, wait. I see. Mrs. Banner."

"Let me see that." She held out her hand, and Safi gave her the notebook. "Thanks." She read the page.

"Mark. Look at this."

She handed the notebook to me. I frowned at the entry that had attracted her attention.

"You saw her get out of a car?"

He took it back. "Yes. The car was silver. I didn't know what kind. I'm still learning about cars."

"You've written down the licence number. CDEF 069. Is that right? And she got home at three forty-two?"

He showed me his wristwatch, a boy's Timex. "I always keep a good battery in it, and I check it against the weather channel on the television every morning."

"You wrote down that a man was driving. You didn't see him?"

"No. Sorry. Otherwise I would have put down a description."

"Mrs. Banner got out of the car, went into her house, and the car drove away."

"Yes."

Rosemary took the book back and brought out her phone. She photographed the page and the two pages following it. "You ever see this car before?"

He shook his head.

"Did Mrs. Banner ever get rides home before?"

He shrugged. "Not that I ever saw. I'm not outside every day, though."

"Almost every day," Sulafa said.

"Was the car noisy? Maybe a bad muffler or something?"

"No."

I looked at Malakia. "If the police come around to talk to you about this, will it be a problem?"

Sulafa and Safi exchanged looks.

"Papa won't be happy," Sulafa said.

"It will be all right," Malakia said. "If you can help them, you must, Safi."

Safi nodded. "Okay, mama."

Rosemary abruptly stood up. "Come on, Mark. Let's go talk to Patrick."

CHAPTER

Forty-Three

We found Patrick in his office, hunched over his keyboard, with a small black-and-white tuxedo cat draped around his neck like a fur stole. It was fast asleep.

"Just a sec," he said, typing madly.

The cat cracked its eyes open, gave us a look, and went back to sleep.

"There." He quit typing and leaned back. "Sorry, a little busy. Got some copy to review and send back for rewrites, but this—he gestured at the screen—is the next installment of the disappearances story. I'm going to run it this week, suggesting a connection among them. What have you got?"

"I sent you a pic," Rosemary said. "What do you think?"

"Sorry. I heard the ping but didn't check. Give me a sec." He pulled out his phone, navigated to it, and stared. "Holy crap. Where did you get this?"

Rosemary told him the story, leaving out Safi's name for the moment.

"We should see if the police have this information," I

said.

"I agree."

"I'm not talking to them," Rosemary said flatly.

"Neither am I," I said. "Shepard already thinks I'm psychotic and his number one suspect."

Patrick shrugged and picked up his landline. "Process of elimination, eh?" He punched in a number. "No worries. Gives me an excuse to ask him again for a statement."

As the call went through, he said, "I'll leave it off speaker."

That was definitely fine by me.

When his call was answered, Patrick asked for Shepard. We were all somewhat surprised when the detective came on the line.

"Yeah, Detective Constable. I'm calling for a couple of reasons. I—"

He rolled his eyes. "I know, but she hasn't returned any of my calls. She must be swamped right now."

He listened. "Okay, look. I want to pass on a piece of information one of my sources—"

He smiled. "I don't reveal the identity of sources, Detective. Give me a second, will you? Thanks. We've discovered that on March 20, two days before her disappearance, Lucy Banner accepted a ride home from someone apparently not seen on that street before. I wanted to know if you already knew about it."

He glanced at me and raised his eyebrows. "Certainly, yeah. It's, uh, CDEF 069. Yeah, that's correct. The source described it as a silver car, no make or model. Showed up at three forty-two, let her off, and drove away. Hmm? A man, yeah. The twentieth, yeah."

He gave Shepard a moment before saying, "I'll call you later to follow up. No, I'll call you, detective. Well, look.

I'll tell you if you give me a comment on something else. Yeah? Hold the line a sec."

He covered the phone and looked at Rosemary. "Name and address."

"Damn."

"It could be really important, Rosie."

She spat out Safi's information.

Patrick repeated it. "A small boy, yeah. I don't know. Now, about that other thing before you go. Do you have any comment now on the possible connection among the four disappearances? Hm? Are you sure that's what you want me to go with? What? Because I'm running the story this week." He laughed. "Well, consider this your heads-up, Detective Shepard. Yeah. I—"

Patrick put down the phone. "He hung up on me. Anyway, mission accomplished. I could tell it was new to him, even though he did his best to sound hard-boiled and disinterested. Who is this kid, anyway?"

"They're a family of Syrian refugees."

"Think he'd talk to me?"

"He might. He's a really smart little kid. Like a little junior detective."

Patrick nodded. "All right. I'm up to my ass in work, so I'm going to give Shepard a bit of time to check it out. I'll call him in the morning. If he stonewalls, I'll go see Safi myself."

The tuxedo cat stirred and jumped down onto the desk, evidently having grown tired of Patrick's yakking. It skidded on a pile of printouts, knocked over an empty Coke can, and jumped down onto the floor.

"What's her name?" I asked, watching the cat stroll nonchalantly out of the office.

"Sabrina. Want her?"

"Is she up for adoption?"

"They all are, Mark. I have no idea where they're all coming from."

I faced the same dilemma with a cat, of course, that I did with a dog. If it outlived me, what would happen to it? I'd never owned a cat before, but I had nothing against them. And I did occasionally find mouse droppings in the house, in places I'd rather that they not end up.

"How old?"

Patrick frowned. "Uh, let's see. I think that one's about two. Jane takes them to the vet to be neutered and to get their shots, so she could tell you for sure, but I think that's right."

"Is she a mouser?"

Patrick grinned. "Aren't they all? Especially the females. Relentless."

"I'll think about it," I said.

CHAPTER

Forty-Four

I don't often watch television, but tonight I'd turned it on to watch *Vertigo*, the Alfred Hitchcock classic starring James Stewart. It had been a number of years since I'd seen it, but I could clearly remember Stewart's obsession with the woman played by Kim Novak, and I wanted to see it again.

I must have dozed off around the time that Stewart had followed Novak to an art museum, where she spent her time staring at a portrait of a woman named Carlotta. When the telephone woke me up, Stewart was well into his obsessive behaviour, insisting that Novak in her "Judy" persona change her clothing and hair to match her appearance to her "Madeleine" persona. I muted the volume and looked at the call display.

"Hello, Patrick."

"You okay, Mark? You sound a little faint."

I sat up straighter in my recliner and cleared my throat. "No, no. I'm fine. What's up?"

"Believe it or not, I just got off the phone with Constable Malloy."

"Who?"

"Kim Malloy, the person Shepard fobbed me off onto for a comment. She actually called *me*."

"Astounding." I found the cup of coffee I'd left on the end table and swallowed a mouthful. Cold, but it hit the spot.

"It seems Shepard followed up on our tip after all. He visited Safi, talked to the family, checked out the notebook, asked a bunch of questions. He'd already run the plate. It came back to a company named Collins Insurance, which is run by a man named Richard Torbert. Allison Banner's older brother."

"Insurance?"

"Yeah. A company car. Shepard called the brother up and talked to him. He remembered picking up Lucy, although he couldn't remember the exact day or date, because Allison had asked him to take her to a doctor's appointment. He said he doesn't often drive the company car, but he must have done so that day."

"I see."

"Malloy didn't say, and Shepard wouldn't bother telling her, but I'm willing to bet that Safi wasn't out on his front step when Torbert picked up Mrs. Banner earlier, but definitely was there when he dropped her off."

"Another false alarm."

"Looks like."

"Damn."

"Yeah. Are you sure you're okay? Do you want me to send Rosie around to check on you?"

"Good God, no. I'm fine. Just tired."

We ended the call and I sat there, staring at the TV without restoring the sound. Something had been running through my head while I dozed. I grasped for the thread, and all I could come up with was that there was something bothering me about the people I'd talked to recently. Something they had in common. I couldn't put my finger on it. I couldn't even remember who the people were I'd been thinking about.

I turned off the television and decided to go upstairs and read in bed for a while.

I went into the kitchen and fixed myself a cup of caffeine-free tea. Not chamomile, because the taste of it always reminded me of the smell of hay. Instead, I picked a cinnamon-rooibos blend that had a nice aroma and an even better flavour. I turned off all the downstairs lights and took it up with me.

I picked out a book I'd bought a while ago at the bookstore but hadn't yet gotten around to reading. It was called *The Alchemist*, by Paulo Coelho. Originally published in Portuguese in 1988, it was a sort of fabulation about a shepherd boy who travels from Spain to Egypt to find an incredible treasure hidden at the pyramids. It turned out to have a charming and engaging tone to it that kept me reading until I'd gone almost a third of the way through.

At some point around there, I fell asleep.

CHAPTER

Forty-Five

I woke up a few minutes after seven o'clock the next morning. The bedside light was still on. I sat up on the side of the bed and instantly knew what it was I'd been trying to put my finger on last evening.

Tattoos.

The baseball scout, Lee Fogarty, had had a tattoo, and so did Bryan Nolan. Sure, tattoos were exceedingly common in this day and age, but there was something about them that was important. And beyond that, some other mental step I had to take.

In the shower, I closed my eyes and pictured the ink on Bryan's arms. There was a flaming skull, the Harley-Davidson logo with an eye above it, a Grim Reaper, and a raven. There were other, smaller, tattoos that I couldn't remember. Hopefully they weren't the kind people got when they killed someone.

While I was eating breakfast, the raven tattoo suddenly generated another memory. Someone else with a raven tattoo. And a fish. And a . . . raccoon?

Who the hell was it?

As I was stacking the dishes into the dishwasher, Bryan's stuffed raven popped into my head. Automatically I was sitting in the doctor's waiting room, talking to Christine Clement, when the maintenance guy came out from the inner office and I stared at the tattoos on his arm: a raccoon, a deer's head, a fish, and a raven.

I picked up the phone and called Rosemary.

"What is it?" her voice was thick and raspy.

"Rosemary, it's Mark. I'm sorry, did I wake you?"

"What do you want?"

"That's all right, I'll call back later."

She grunted. "What time is it?"

"Eight forty-two."

"Jesus."

"How about I call back at ten?"

A pause. "Nah, it's all right. Give me a minute, will you?"

I listened to rustling and fumbling, then the snicking of a lighter. Then a long, protracted Rosemary sigh. "What do you want?"

"Something occurred to me this morning. We've seen a couple of people with tattoos, and it got me thinking. Where did Bryan get his done?"

"What difference does it make?" She coughed out smoke. "Gawd. Agh. Hell, Mark, I've got tattoos, for chrissakes."

"I never noticed."

"Yeah, well, they're some place you're not supposed to look, grandpa."

"Don't call me that. Fogarty, the baseball guy, has a tattoo, and so does that maintenance guy at the clinic. Martin. Who does them around here?"

"Just a minute."

The phone clunked and I heard her walking away.

There was silence for over a minute. I waited it out. A toilet flushed and a tap ran. Footsteps grew louder. There was fumbling.

"Quarter to nine in the frigging morning. I thought you old geezers always slept in."

"Early bird gets the worm, Rosemary."

"Whatever the hell that means. Bryan got most of his tatts done years ago. Before he retired. Right after the pandemic he got one of a heart and Faith Ann. On his leg. I went to the same guy for mine."

"Who's that?"

"Dude named Josh Beam. He's got a shop in town. On Foster."

"How can I find out whether this Martin character got his there, too?"

"Call and ask him. Josh is a pretty good guy."

"He's not going to talk to me about other customers."

"Say the guy recommended you to him."

I thought about it for a moment. It was worth a try. "I'll let you know what I find out."

"Do that."

"Should I wait until ten to call you back?"

"He's probably not open until ten, Mark."

"I'll look him up. What's the place called?"

"On the Beam Tattoos and Piercings."

"I'll call you back after ten."

"Whenever. I'm up now. Time for a caffeine hit. Later."

When I Googled the business name, I saw that it had opened at nine, so I called.

"On the Beam. What's happening?"

"Yeah, this is Mark. I'm thinking of getting a tattoo, and a guy I know, Martin, recommended you."

"Is that so. Martin who?"

"Martin with tattoos of raccoons, fishes, and ravens."

"That clown. Yeah. Are you as fucking nutzoid as he is?"

"I hope not. What about a guy named Lee Fogarty?"

"Never heard of him. What's this about? Are you a cop or something?"

"Just wanted to know if I can trust Martin's recommendation."

"My work's the best in eastern Ontario, man. What kind of art are you thinking about?"

"Actually, I've changed my mind. Thanks." I cut the call and put down the phone.

So what on earth did I know now that I didn't know last night?

CHAPTER

Forty-Six

I called Rosemary back and told her I was picking her up for lunch. I took her to a little sandwich place on a side street downtown, and we sat on high stools at the window counter to eat our BLTs, watching birds hop around on the sidewalk, busily chasing up their own chow.

She didn't look very well. I didn't say too much as she worked her way through one half of the sandwich, but when she slowed down and began picking at the bacon in the second half, I wiped my fingers on my napkin and put my elbows on the counter.

"Your tattoo guy, Josh Beam, also did the work we saw on Martin the maintenance man."

She examined a sliver of bacon and put it in her mouth. "So?"

"So that's one guy we haven't looked at yet."

She was silent for a while, staring out at the street. "I couldn't sleep last night." She'd told me before she never drank, and it didn't look exactly like a hangover, so I figured she wasn't kidding when she said she hadn't slept.

"He's dead, isn't he?"

"Probably."

"Yeah." She looked down at her plate. "I keep going over and over it. I should've done this different, should've done that different. Maybe he's still alive. Maybe I can still find him. But I know. I *know*. In my heart. He's dead. It's too late."

"At this point," I said, "our most important job is to find the guy who's doing it so he doesn't do it again."

"Save some other poor person. Somebody he's probably scoping out right now, waiting for the right moment to swoop in like a goddamned vulture."

No, vultures eat dead things, I thought. *The next one's still alive.* Then I thought, dead things. Stuffed animals in Bryan's shop. Dead things. The same dead animals that were on display in the garage were tattooed to Martin's arms. Raccoon; fish; deer head; raven.

"What's the name of Bryan's taxidermist?"

"How the fuck should I know?"

"It could be important. Another connection."

"I hate those damned things. Dead animals with their guts pulled out and pillow stuffing shoved in. They give me the creeps."

"Can you find out who he uses? He talked to me about the guy but never said his name. Can you call him and ask?"

She gave me a look. "Right now? I'm not going to call him now. It's his day off. He's probably still in bed."

"It could be important," I repeated.

She closed her eyes for a moment, chewing on her bottom lip. "Take me home."

"Okay." I wrapped up the rest of my sandwich.

"We'll talk to him there," she said.

CHAPTER

Forty-Seven

When we got back to Rosemary's trailer, Bryan was tooling around on his riding lawnmower, cutting the grass. She flagged him down and explained that we needed to have a word with him. He nodded, shut off the machine, and went inside the house. Rosemary and I sat down at her picnic table to wait. After a few moments he came out with a can of beer in one hand and a towel in the other.

He sat down next to Rosemary, across from me, and wiped the perspiration from his forehead and face. "What's up?"

"I wanted to ask you who your taxidermist is," I said.

He rubbed the back of his neck with the towel. "Why?"

"I don't know," I admitted. "I guess I'm fishing. Pun intended. First it was the tattoos. Rosemary and I saw a guy with tattoos that matched the stuffed animals in your shop. I'm trying to figure out if it's important."

"You're probably talking about Hadley." He put down the towel and drank about half the can in one gulp.

"He's got this thing about getting tattoos of the animals he stuffs," he continued. Some weird shit there. Beam won't take his business any more." He looked at Rosemary. "I don't think you ever saw him, did you?"

"The taxidermist? Nope."

"I used to use an old guy named McParland," he said to me, "lived out in Stanleyville. I think I mentioned him to you before. When he croaked, like I said, his business was turned over to this kid who apprenticed with him. He's pretty good. Did a really good job on the raven, which was a bit mangled up after getting hit by the car."

"His name's Hadley?"

"Yeah. Martin Hadley."

I looked at Rosemary.

"Martin," she said.

"Why?" Bryan repeated. "What's this got to do with anything?"

"We're not sure," I said, "but there's a connection between him and the mother of a woman who disappeared a year ago. Emily Clement. Where can we find him, Bryan?"

"I don't know where he does his work. He uses his mother's house as a pick-up and drop-off point. On Paterson Street."

"Where on Paterson?" Rosemary asked.

"Four twelve. Crappy little bungalow." He drained the can and stood up. "Anything else?"

"No," I said. "Thanks for your help."

We watched him toss the can into Rosemary's recycling bin and stride across to his lawnmower.

"We should go check this guy out," Rosemary said.

"Do you feel up to it?"

She put her head down in her arms. "I feel like crap. I need about four hours' sleep."

"I can go see him. You don't need to be there."

"All right," she said. "See ya later."

CHAPTER

Forty-Eight

The house on Paterson Street was set back from the road. A walkway made of cracked and uneven patio stones led up to an enclosed front porch. At first, I thought the lawn was one of those no-maintenance alternative landscapes that were becoming popular these days, with tall flowering weeds, fallen branches for organic mulch, untrimmed shrubs, and other wild growth. Halfway up the walk I decided it was more likely that no one had cut the grass or picked up the debris since the snow had disappeared. Neglect, pure and simple.

On my right was a driveway leading to a fallen-down garage. Parked in front of the garage was a white van. There were no windows on the back or sides. From where I stood, I could see traces of the Butler Brothers Janitorial Services logo that had been painted over. I recognized the rust spots and dents from having sketched the vehicle when it was parked outside the clinic last Sunday.

I rapped on the outer door of the house. No response. I tried the latch. The door opened, so I stepped inside the porch and rapped on the inner door. After a moment I heard heavy footsteps, and a woman opened up and stared out at me.

Somewhere in her fifties, she wore a flowered dress and a light green apron. Her house slippers had fur around the edges. Her grey hair was short and held back at the temples with bobby pins. The bags under her eyes had bags of their own, and her front teeth protruded through thick lips.

"Yes?"

"Is this where Martin Hadley lives?"

"Who wants to know?"

"My name's Mark Heron. I'm hoping to be able to talk to Martin, if he's here."

"You a cop?"

I laughed, as though scandalized. "Hardly. Is he here? May I come in?"

She held the door for me. I stood in the hallway and she disappeared. Several minutes passed. The house had a pleasant smell to it, mixed odours of cleaning liquids, fresh air from an open window somewhere, baked pastry, and floor wax. It was completely silent.

I concentrated on the smells, on feeling faint air currents passing across my cheeks, and the sound of a vehicle passing in the street. I remained standing but tried to keep my muscles loose and relaxed. I became conscious of my breathing and kept it slow and deep.

Eventually I heard footsteps crossing above my head. Someone thumped down the stairs.

Martin Hadley stopped and stared at me. "What do you want?"

"We met in Dr. Stevenson's office a while ago. A friend of mine and I were talking to Mrs. Clement."

"I remember seeing you, yeah. What do you want?"

"Can we sit down for a minute and talk?"

"About what?"

"I wouldn't mind a glass of water," I said.

"Go in there." He pointed through a doorway to a sitting room and walked away.

I went in and sat down on the couch. The room was gloomy, with heavy drapes pulled across the windows, but it was clean and tidy. I expected another long wait, but he came in and handed me a tumbler of water and stood over me, hands on his hips.

"Thanks." I took a drink. I'd stood in the hall a little bit longer than was physically comfortable for me, and I was glad for the water, which was refreshing. He was still looming over me. "Please, sit down. This won't take long."

He sat in a chair across from me and folded his hands in his lap.

I looked at the tattoos that were fully visible beneath the cuffs of his plain black T-shirt. "I'm looking for someone who might be able to do a bit of taxidermy work for me. Bryan Nolan says he's a customer of yours."

"Bryan. Yeah. What've you got?"

"Hm?"

"What do you want stuffed?"

"Oh. A fish. A muskie."

"How big?"

"About forty-five inches."

"Nice. Where'd you get it?"

"The Ottawa River. Near Arnprior." I was amazed at how proficient a liar I was becoming. I'd overheard two men in the McDonald's one Friday talking about their respective fishing trips, and the details had stuck in the back of my head.

"Good fishing up there. When do you want it done?"

"I can bring it to your workshop tomorrow. Where is it?"

He shook his head. "Bring it here. When I'm done, I'll call you and you can pick it up here."

"Isn't it easier if I just deliver it right to your shop?"

"That isn't how it works. Take it or leave it."

"Okay." I drained the glass of water and put it down. "You seem to know Mrs. Clement pretty well."

He shrugged. "We talk. I know a lot of the people who work in the offices."

"It was too bad about her daughter."

"Yeah. She was there sometimes. The daughter."

I saw an expression cross his face that surprised me. "You didn't like her? Emily?"

"She was a bitch. She had a bad attitude. She was disrespectful to her mother."

"Oh. I didn't know that."

"I feel bad for Mrs. Clement, though. She's all alone now."

I frowned. "How do you know that?"

"She talks to me sometimes." He shrugged again. "She's a lonely person."

I was starting to feel uncomfortable, almost claustrophobic. He radiated sickness in palpable waves. I reminded myself that people with mental health challenges were everywhere, and the fact that he was clearly unwell didn't mean he had anything to do with the disappearances of Nathan Notwell or Emily Clement or the other people.

"Is that your van in the driveway?" I asked, to change the subject.

"Yes. They let me buy it. I never had a car before. I always had to get rides to work."

"Who let you buy it?"

"Mr. Butler and his brother. They were going to get rid of it, but Lance, he's my supervisor, got them to sell it to me instead. They even had it painted for me."

"How's it run?"

"Okay. I hit a bad pothole though and wrecked the muffler. I gotta get that fixed some time."

I held my breath for a moment. A bad muffler made for a noisy vehicle, and a noisy vehicle was a thread running through this investigation.

"Ever drive around Centennial Park, Martin? Or the streets around there?"

He shook his head. "Why would I?"

"Do you have a girlfriend?"

"Yeah, she's a *Tik Tok* star. My friends are all jealous."

"Have you—"

He stood up abruptly. "It's time for you to get out."

"I'm sorry. I didn't mean to offend you."

He grabbed the shoulder of my shirt and pulled. "Up. Out."

"Hey, none of that now. All right, I'm leaving." I got to my feet and quickly left the house.

I sat in the Escalade without starting the engine. I realized I was shaking. I took a drink of water from the bottle in the centre console and tried to calm down. I'd come close to being physically assaulted. If I'd resisted when he pulled on my shoulder, if I'd knocked his hand away, I'm sure he would have hit me.

Something banged on the window next to my ear, scaring me half to death.

It was him, staring in at me.

I started the engine and lowered the window a crack. Enough to hear him, but not enough for him to reach in.

"I think you better stay away from me from now on,"

he said.

"Why? What did I do wrong?"

"Just stay away, or I may have to hurt you. Really hurt you."

"Are you threatening me?"

He closed his hand into a fist and pressed it against the window. "Just stay away from me."

CHAPTER

Forty-Nine

Let me just say for the record that I'm not a physical coward. It's true I don't like confrontations and will avoid them whenever possible, especially now that I've reached a certain age and I'm not quite as confident as I used to be about being able to hold my own in a dust-up, but I'm not a coward. Like many people, when I'm threatened I tend toward the front half of the fight-or-flight response.

When I rolled out of bed the next morning, my blood was still roiled. I kept thinking of things I should have said to the punk to put him in his place. I chided myself that there was probably evidence of Martin Hadley' guilt sitting in plain sight that I could have spotted if I'd handled myself better.

After dinner last night I'd tried calling Rosemary to update her, but her phone kept going straight to voicemail, so after a while I gave up and went upstairs to read in bed. Eventually I dozed off, and that was it.

For once, I slept right through.

I had a quick breakfast and tried Rosemary's number again. When she answered, there was a lot of noise in the background, and she had to shout to be heard.

"I'm on my way to work! Are you all right?"

"You're driving? On your bike?"

"Yeah!"

"That's dangerous. You should pull over."

"Relax, Mark! It's hands-free, built right into the helmet. Didn't I show you that before?"

"Maybe you did."

"I work until one, and then I'm coming over! Will you be there?"

"I'll be here."

The line went dead.

At twenty minutes after one o'clock, she pulled in and parked behind the Escalade. Assuming her favourite spot on the top step, her back against the railing post, she lit a cigarette and squinted at me through the smoke.

"I was a little worried about you last night. I saw that you'd called a bunch of times and when I called back it went to voice mail."

"Did you leave a message?" I hadn't noticed the little light flashing on the handsets to let me know that one had been left.

"Nah. I figured you were already asleep."

"I guess I was. I didn't hear the phone ring." I put the ashtray down where she could get at it.

"So what were you calling about?"

I paused, reminding myself not to get overly dramatic or too wound up again. "I talked to Martin Hadley."

"Sorry I couldn't go with you. It's the same guy we saw at the clinic?"

"The same guy. Drives a crappy old white van that I'm willing to bet makes a lot of noise. He said the muffler was damaged on it."

"So what else did he say?"

"Weird things. I can see why Beam doesn't like him and won't do his tattoos any more. It's like his brain's miswired." I rocked slowly back and forth in the rocking chair. "For one thing, he'd met Emily Clement before, when she visited her mother at the office, and he didn't like her. He called her a bitch and said she was disrespectful to her mother."

Rosemary snorted. "Is that so? Well, according to the uncle, she was just fine. No problems. Sampson's a doorknob, but I'd believe what he says over some goofball maintenance guy."

"He got upset with me when I asked if he had a girlfriend. He threw me out."

She raised her eyebrows but said nothing.

"He got a little physical about it."

"Shit. What happened?"

"He grabbed me and pulled me up out of the chair. I think he was almost ready to hit me."

Rosemary angrily stubbed out her cigarette. "Son of a bitch. You don't have to take that kind of bullshit. Let's go over there and explain the facts of life to him."

I smiled faintly. She certainly was feeling protective of me lately. Driving over after work to make sure I was all right, and now willing to pound some sense into Martin Hadley. A far cry from the Rosemary who'd flipped me the bird in the grocery store and told me to fuck off.

"He's hostile," I said, "so we need to keep our distance."

"Not if he may be the guy who took Nathan. Not a chance."

"I've been trying to think this through. There's got to be a way to get more on him."

She lit another cigarette. "I'm getting tired of these guys not panning out. What's his name, Follett, with the restraining order on him. The old river rat, O'Toole. Dollar Man Sampson. Fogarty, the baseball guy. Lucy's uncle, driving her home. Any one of them could have been the one, and none of them is. Christ, it's frustrating."

"Yeah." I watched her stare at the blue spruces along the driveway, cigarette between her long, bony fingers. Something she'd just said had nudged something else in my head. I worked on it for a moment, and then I had it.

"Let's take a drive past Hadley's place and take a few pictures of his van."

"I thought you just said we should stay clear."

"Of him. But not necessarily his van."

She curled her lip. "Okay, so we take a pic of his vehicle. What for? So we can give it to Patrick so he can give it to Shepard so he can ignore it?"

"No, I know a better person we could show it to."

"Who the hell's that?"

"Think about it, Rosemary. If Martin Hadley snatched Lucy Banner, it's more than likely he was checking her out beforehand, right? Learning her schedule and her habits, trying to find the best opportunity to grab her."

"Sure, but—" She stopped in her tracks and stared at me. "Are you thinking what I'm thinking?"

I smiled. "Let's take that picture and show it to Safi."

CHAPTER

Fifty

Easier said than done, because first we had to track down Martin Hadley so we could photograph his van.

We drove into town, but the van was not parked at his mother's house. I went up to the door and knocked, hoping Mrs. Hadley could tell us where her son was, but there was no answer.

We looked up the address of Butler Brothers and discovered it was headquartered in a rezoned two-storey frame house on the far edge of town. When we arrived, we saw a couple of their vehicles parked in front, and when I rolled through the lot, we spotted Martin's white van around the side next to a secondary exit.

I stopped and got out. The door was wedged open, and the side door of the van was rolled back. I looked in at buckets and mops, a plastic garbage can, a vacuum cleaner, and other paraphernalia of the trade.

"What the hell are you doing?"

I swung around, startled. Martin Hadley was standing in the doorway, a bucket of Borax in his hand.

"We didn't exactly finish our talk, Martin."

"Yes, we did." He carried the bucket to his van, put it inside, and slid the door shut. Then he pivoted and punched me in the stomach.

I went down like a burst balloon.

I've always hated the feeling that comes with having the wind knocked out of me. The few times I'd played sports as a kid I'd almost invariably ended up on the ground, curled up in a fetal position, gasping for air. It felt like I was dying. I needed to inhale, but I couldn't.

This was it. I couldn't breathe. Agony. Panic!

I rolled over onto my back and raised my legs. There. A tiny breath.

I was aware of the van starting, its noisy engine roaring in my ear. I saw its front wheel begin to roll past my head. It swivelled as I lay there, gasping shallow little hiccups, and I knew that Martin was turning the van. I watched the wheel move in a short arc toward my head.

Air was still my top priority, but it occurred to me he might be trying to run me over. He intended to crush my head like a pumpkin.

Suddenly I was being dragged clear. Rosemary gave me a quick look and bolted after the van, which was roaring out of the parking lot.

"Come back here, asshole!" she shouted.

I managed to roll over onto my side, and then onto my hands and knees. Suddenly Rosemary was there, pulling on my arm, hauling me to my feet.

"Are you all right? Son of a bitch! Are you all right?"

"I'm fine," I wheezed, brushing at grit on the front of my shirt. "Just my . . . wind." I disengaged my arm from hers and bent over, hands on my knees. I gagged, spat, and groaned. "Christ, I hate this." I straightened up. "Tell me you got it."

"Sure. Video of him hitting you, getting in the van, and trying to run you over. It gets bouncy after that. I shut it off while I was running to save your sorry old ass."

"Thanks, by the way."

"No problem. You still want to show it to Safi?"

"Now more than ever."

"You want me to drive?"

"No, I'm good."

We climbed in and I started the engine.

"I thought you said we should steer clear of him."

"Yeah." I looked at the dashboard clock. It was ten minutes past three o'clock in the afternoon. "Safi may still be in school."

"Let's go anyway. We should talk to his parents."

"You're right."

I drove slowly, and as we approached the middle of town I pulled into the Tim Hortons drive-through and bought myself a cup of coffee. Rosemary had a bagel sandwich and a large Coke.

"I didn't eat lunch," she said, thanking me.

By the time we reached Safi's street, Rosemary had finished her sandwich and was wiping her fingers on her napkin. I glanced at the clock again. It was a few minutes before three thirty.

We passed Lucy Banner's place.

We're coming, I thought. *We'll find you.*

The children were not yet home from school, so Rosemary and I sat down for another glass of sweet tea with Mrs. Nahas at the kitchen table.

"I understand the police came by to talk to Safi," I said. "Did it go all right?"

"Yes. They were polite and kind to him. The police have been here before. Not those detectives, but other officers.

They were part of the welcoming committee assembled by the church group that sponsored us."

"Sometimes they're less than patient with recent immigrants."

"Compared to the Taliban, they were perfect gentlemen."

"Not that it's especially relevant," I said, "but my ancestors were also immigrants to this country, several generations ago."

"I see."

"When I was a younger man, I hired a professional genealogist to trace my roots. It seems my Heron family came to Canada from County Armagh in Ireland, descending from the sept referred to in Irish Gaelic as *O HEarain*, meaning 'dread' or 'dreadful.' Interesting. I prefer the alternative story, that the family was named after the species of bird. At any rate, Irish Catholic settlers were not often made welcome by their Protestant counterparts, who'd already received government grants for the best land and had already established themselves in the township hierarchies. It's a long and depressing tale."

"But your family eventually integrated into the Canadian way of life," she said.

"In our case, assimilated would be more accurate. But I'm hopeful that you folks will find a smoother path forward for your children and grandchildren."

We heard the door open, and Safi trotted into the kitchen, tossing his knapsack on a chair. "I knew you were here. I saw your car."

"It's those skills of observation Rosemary and I want to take advantage of again."

"Sure. Same date?"

"Same notebook."

He grinned at his mother and pulled out a cupboard drawer. "I thought so. I kept it down here, just in case."

"Have a seat," Rosemary said, pulling a chair over next to her. "Take a look at this first." She held out her phone and thumbed the video clip of Hadley and his van into life.

Safi nodded. "That's the one." Then he looked at me. "He hit you!"

"The licence plate's visible here," Rosemary said, pointing.

Safi continued to watch. "Yes. This is it. The one I saw." He opened his notebook, flipping pages. "I saw it every day for more than a week. Here."

Rosemary reached for it, but he held it away. "Let me find the first entry first. Then you call follow it forward. Just a sec. Here."

She took it and ran her finger down the page. "Okay. Wednesday, March 14. White van. Two entries: three fifty-one and six twenty-six. Westbound both times."

"Did he stop in front of her place?"

"I guess not, or I would have written it down."

"Okay." Rosemary turned the page. "Here. Next day. White van, a man driving, the same licence plate. Four twelve in the afternoon."

"Yes," Safi said.

"Then you say he went down to the corner and turned right." She looked at me. "I wonder if he was cruising the next street over, checking their back yard."

"Could be," I said.

Rosemary pointed. "This is Mrs. Banner, is it?"

"Yes. She always parks in the little driveway beside her house."

"Small blue car. This is the licence number."

"Yes."

Rosemary turned more pages.

Safi had recorded three more sightings of the white van. Rosemary took photos of each page before looking at me.

"Shepard needs to see these."

I nodded.

"I'll send them to Patrick."

I stood up. "Thank you very much, Safi. I think you'll be getting another visit from Detective Constable Shepard."

"Okay."

I looked at his mother.

She nodded, although her eyes were worried.

CHAPTER

Fifty-One

I drove Rosemary home and left her with the task of forwarding the new images of Safi's notebooks to Patrick, who, we agreed, was the best conduit right now to get the information through to Detective Constable Shepard.

I was tired. The day had taken a lot out of me, not to mention the punch in the stomach from a punk quite a few decades younger than I was. My midsection was still sore and my legs still a bit shaky.

I ate a light dinner and went outside to my favourite spot in times of need—the rocking chair on my front verandah. I took a book out with me that had been a big deal when I was at college—a volume of poetry by Michael Ondaatje called *The Collected Works of Billy the Kid*—but I began to doze after only a few pages and I set it aside so it wouldn't slip out of my fingers and drop to the verandah floor, scaring the crap out of me while I was trying to snooze.

Some time later, I awoke to the sound of a noisy vehicle on the road. Dusk had arrived, and the porch light came on as I stirred. Only half-conscious, I wondered if Rosemary was stopping in for a visit. The rumbling slowed at the end of my driveway. I closed my eyes for a moment, hoping for a few more seconds of dozing time.

A smashing sound, followed by a *whooshh,* brought me fully awake. I sat up abruptly as a second crash and *whooshh* ensued.

Trouble!

I bolted from the rocking chair and clattered down the stairs in my carpet slippers as light suddenly flared at the end of the driveway and the vehicle roared away, back toward town.

I ran past the Escalade and toward the road, only to stop dead at the sight of the blue spruce trees closest to the road engulfed in flames on each side of the driveway. They burned like giant cones of fire, hissing and sparking as the resin in the branches and needles ignited and flared.

I took a few steps forward, as though there were something I might be able to do, but quickly realized it was out of control. I turned and ran back inside the house to call 911.

To their credit, the township fire department arrived at the scene in less than fifteen minutes. By that time, though, the fires had spread to the next tree in each row. As I watched in horror, I feared they would all be lost and my house would be in danger. Thank goodness at least for a tin roof that rejected drifting sparks and white-hot particles.

Dark smoke and an acrid smell filled the air as they hosed down the trees while I talked to the fire chief, a man named Bob Chambers. I explained what I'd heard, not bothering to hide the fact that I'd been asleep in the rocking chair like a dotard. I started to talk about Martin Hadley and his white van, but at that point someone approached us from the direction of the field, having parked along the road to skirt the driveway, the burning trees, and the fire vehicles.

It was Shepard.

"You're having another little adventure, I see."

"I seem to be, although they're getting it under control now, thank God."

"So tell me what happened."

I went through it again, this time emphasizing the loud engine noise and my belief that Martin Hadley was responsible. I also mentioned the recent altercations with him, and went on to talk about Safi and his documentation of the presence of the white van on Lucy's street the week before her disappearance.

He let me ramble on, and when I finally came up for air, he folded his arms and nodded. "Your journalist friend sent me the new images of the boy's notebook. We ran the plate and it came back to Martin Hadley, so that part of your new theory is correct."

Man, I didn't like this guy's tone. "New theory." So sarcastic.

"We sent a car around to pick him up for questioning," he went on, "but his mother didn't know where he was." He shrugged. "We brought her in. So far, nothing."

"Whatever it is he's doing, he doesn't seem to be doing it there."

"We also brought your girlfriend in and got the story from her about today's fun and games."

"How many times do I have to tell you she's not my girlfriend? She's young enough to be my granddaughter, for chrissakes."

I saw the lines deepen at the corners of his eyes and realized he was just ragging me.

"We'll find him," he said. "It's only a matter of time.

Listen, did you get yourself checked out at the hospital after he beat you up?"

"No. It wasn't necessary. And it was only one punch."

"Any signs of blood? In your mucus or urine?"

"I'm fine. Really. I'm tougher than I look."

"All right." He looked up the driveway at the remains of the conflagration. "They'll have to be cut down."

"I know. The burned ones, anyway."

"I don't normally handle arson. Give your full co-operation to the detective when she gets here, okay?"

"Will do."

"And stay out of this. I don't want you hurt any more than you already have been. Please, let the professionals handle it from here. It's why we get paid the big bucks."

I gave him my best drawn-out Rosemary sigh and nodded.

CHAPTER

Fifty-Two

Of course, I ended up doing no such thing.

On Tuesday a guy from a tree removal service came around to give me an estimate on cutting down and taking away the burned spruces. The front two trees on the west side would have to go, and while the third was a bit scorched and might drop some needles, it could stay for now. On the east side, the front tree was toast. The second one was half-intact, but after a bit of dithering I told him to remove it, as well. He gave me a price, and I agreed to it. He said they'd be able to come out the next morning to get the job done.

In the afternoon, Larry Wilson came around to talk to me. Larry, you may recall, was Patrick's staff reporter. We sat down on the verandah so that he could interview me. He told me that Constable Kim Malloy had distributed a press release about a person of interest named Martin Hadley who was wanted for questioning in the disappearances of four individuals in the area. They included a description of his vehicle and its licence number, along with a Crime Stoppers number for anyone in the public to call if they saw this man or had any information that could lead to his apprehension.

"About time," I said, still grouchy.

"Yeah. They also had another one, about you getting firebombed. I'm covering that one while Patrick and Dorothy work on the big story."

"Sorry if you're stuck playing second fiddle."

He grinned. "Not at all. 'Local celebrity's property hit with Molotov cocktails'? Complete with pictures? I'll get my column inches, don't worry. We'll just have to squeeze the charity golf tournament onto the back page."

I ran him through the story; he took a photograph of me in the rocking chair holding my signature cigar; and he stopped at the end of the driveway for several shots of the damage before tooling off, a happy man.

Normally it wasn't the kind of publicity I sought, and while I knew there was a good chance it would get picked up by Canadian Press and one or two American newswires, I didn't care. I was pissed. I wanted Hadley caught and punished, and to hell with the rest of it.

On Wednesday morning, the tree service guys showed up, as good as their word, and got to work removing the burned-out hulks of my beloved blue spruces. I went down to make sure the crew understood their instructions, and then went inside. I couldn't stand to watch.

I hid in my studio, reading books of collected cartoons by my peers and drinking hot sweet mint tea, which I'd suddenly discovered I liked very much. I flipped through three volumes of Calvin and Hobbes strips by Bill Watterson without seeing them before my attention was finally caught and held by a handful of paperbacks by Virgil Partch, a.k.a. Vip, whose gags were frequently considered too cheeky for *The New Yorker* but regularly appeared in *Playboy*,

Collier's, and other fine publications.

Eventually the doorbell rang and the tree removal supervisor guy told me they were done, everything had been hauled away, and the office would be sending the invoice out in the next few days. I thanked him and went back to Vip.

After a while I ventured outside. The mouth of my driveway looked as though it were missing four front teeth. I realized I hadn't asked about the stumps. I'd have to think about what to do with them.

As I was walking back into the house, the phone was ringing. It was Rosemary.

"Patrick told me about the fire. Sorry I didn't call earlier. Are you all right?"

"I'm fine, thanks. What are you up to?"

"Are you busy right now?"

"Not at all. What would you like?"

"Can you come and pick me up?"

I frowned. Why would she want me to pick her up? Was her bike out of service? "Sure. Where are you?"

"At the hospital."

She must be visiting someone, I thought. "Who's there?"

"I am, Mark. For God's sake. Can you pick me up?"

My heart jumped. "Is something wrong? Are you okay?

"Just come and get me. I'll tell you when I see you."

She was waiting for me on a bench outside Emergency. I pulled into the circular driveway, shifted into park, and got out. She was a little tentative standing up, but when I put my hand on her arm she shook me off. She let me open the passenger door for her, though, so that was something.

"Take me to your place," she said as I pulled into traffic.

"I don't want to go home right now."

"Okay."

I threaded my way through the town, keeping my mouth shut, and when we were finally onto the highway heading north toward Tennyson Road, she began to talk.

"I saw him. Mark. Hadley. I was visiting Grace, you know, trying to pick her spirits up a bit. When I left, I was sitting at the intersection waiting to turn, and that son of a bitch went right past me."

"Oh my God."

"I took off after him. He was heading up this way, can you believe it? I got close and the bastard hit the brakes. I swerved to avoid rear-ending him and went into the ditch."

"My God, Rosemary. Are you all right?"

"I'm fine. Someone stopped and called 911. I was a little woozy for a few minutes, so the paramedics took me in. They checked me out, x-rays and concussion tests and all the rest of it. I cracked a bone."

She held up her left arm so I could see the tension bandage wrapped around her wrist. "Otherwise, no problems. They wanted me to stay overnight for observation, but I said, 'Fuck that. I gotta get outta here.' When are they going to nail that bastard?"

"Soon, I hope. They put out a lookout on him. If he's driving around somewhere, they'll pick him up soon."

"They better." At that moment, her cellphone rang.

"Yeah? Oh, hi."

It was Bryan. The volume on her phone was turned up loud enough that I could hear both sides of the conversation.

"I called the hospital and they said you were out."

"Yeah, Mark picked me up. I'm going over to his place

for a while."

"I brought your bike back."

"Thanks."

"One of the forks is bent. So's the front wheel. Headlight's broke. Gas tank's dented. It's going to need some work, Rosie."

"Okay. I'll find a way to pay for it."

"You want a loaner?"

"That'd be good."

"It's not a Harley. Is that going to be a problem?"

She snorted. "Beggars can't be choosers."

"It's a 2003 Honda 750. I took it as partial payment for a job last year. Runs okay. We'll put a dealer plate on it."

Rosemary groaned. "A Honda? Are you trying to humiliate me?"

"Take it or leave it, girl."

"Take it. Thanks, cuz."

"No problem."

A few minutes later, her phone rang again.

"I was just talking to Bryan," a baritone voice growled. "Are you all right, kid?"

"Yeah, Bill. I'm okay."

"Do you know who the fucker was?"

"Yeah, but don't worry. I've got it under control."

The voice swore again, and I realized it was probably the guy who'd shown up at Bryan's shop with his nephew. The Outlaws guy.

"Something like this can't be let go."

"I know, Bill. It'll be taken care of. I'm on top of it."

"Let me handle it for you. What's his name? Where do I find him?"

"No, Bill. Please. I gotta do it my way."

"You sure? Nobody messes with friends of mine and

gets away with it."

"Yeah, I know. But thanks for the offer."

"You got my number. If you change your mind."

"I've got it. Thanks."

The line went dead.

She moped the rest of the way to my place.

I got her settled in the wicker chair on the verandah and went in for a Coke. I'd just handed it to her when her cellphone rang again.

"Hey, Grace. What's up?"

Her face grew dark. "I don't understand. Slow down. Who's gone?"

"What? I don't understand you." She put it on speaker.

"Her daughter's gone!" Gracie blurted. "I'm telling you! She called me a few minutes ago. The police are there, and they're talking to her husband. She thinks I know where she is. How would I know? I tried to explain, but she wouldn't listen. She's hysterical."

"Who's gone, Gracie? Make sense. Who the hell are you talking about?"

"Renata Bazuski! Nathan's friend! She's disappeared!"

CHAPTER

Fifty-Three

We argued about what to do. Rosemary wanted to race right over to the Bazuski house to find out exactly what had happened. I resisted, on the grounds that Renata and Martin Hadley would already be long gone, and that the police would be setting up perimeters, conducting door-to-door searches, and watching every side street and driveway for Hadley's van.

Exasperated, Rosemary called Patrick. It went to voicemail. She left a message explaining what had happened and asking him to call her right back.

"We have to do *something!*"

"I know," I said, "but what? What can we do to help?"

"We can drive around, look for Hadley's van, follow him to wherever he's taking these people."

"Drive around at random? We'd be wasting our time. We need to know more before we jump in with both feet."

Rosemary looked at her phone. "There's no point in me calling Gracie again. She's a wreck."

A vehicle went by on the road, coming from the direction of town. The engine was loud and annoying, reminding me that periodically I would hear such a racket passing here, a brief disruption to the peace and quiet. And there it was again, intruding on my thought processes when I needed to concentrate on the current crisis.

Rosemary and I looked down the driveway at the road. Because of the missing trees, we had a better view of the vehicle as it roared by.

It was a white van.

"Christ almighty!" Rosemary yelled. "It's him!"

I still had my keys in my pocket. I raced to the Escalade. "Get in!"

She jumped in the passenger seat with much more alacrity than she'd shown at the hospital, and barely had time to buckle herself in before I was shifting into reverse and backing up the driveway to the road.

I swung out and shifted into drive. The van was still in sight, slowing to make a right-hand turn onto Muldoon Side Road. I floored the accelerator. The big engine roared, and our heads snapped back as we surged forward.

The van turned onto Muldoon. I reached the corner in record time, hit the brakes, fishtailed a bit, and made the turn.

"Be careful!" Rosemary shouted. "Don't kill us!"

She had a point. We'd just left a paved county road for a gravel secondary road, and the Escalade's tires spun as they groped for traction. I lifted my foot off the gas pedal for a moment, using compression to regain control.

The van ran ahead of us, raising a cloud of dust from the gravel and hardpan. I was afraid I was going to lose sight of it, that it would turn off somewhere up ahead and I wouldn't know until we passed the spot and would have to stop and retrace our steps, losing valuable time.

I couldn't believe it, then, when I realized it was slowing

down, its brake lights flaring through the dust.

"What the hell's he doing?"

"I don't know," I said. "The road forks farther ahead. There's only—"

He turned into the driveway of the abandoned house, the one I could see from the rear of my property. I slowed down. The van's rear lights flashed in front of the house as he shifted into park and killed the engine.

I turned in and edged forward.

"He's getting out," Rosemary said, her voice now calm.

I stopped and shut off the engine.

Rosemary opened her door.

"Wait," I said, but she was already closing the door behind her.

I pulled my keys and slid out.

Martin Hadley stood at the end of his van, staring at us. In his hand was a tire iron. "I told you to stay away from me," he said.

Rosemary advanced on him. "Where's Renata, you fucking psycho? Where is she?"

"Wait," I said again, but she wasn't listening. She had Hadley's attention, so I moved forward, hoping to disarm him somehow.

I was two meters away when he suddenly lunged at me, swinging his weapon. I saw it coming at the last moment and twisted enough that it only caught me with a glancing blow across my forehead, but it was sufficiently violent to knock me to the ground. My head rang like a bell.

Before he could recover his balance, however, Rosemary made her move. She stepped up and threw a solid right to the jaw.

Martin Hadley dropped the tire iron and folded to the ground, knocked out by a single punch.

CHAPTER

Fifty-Four

We found Renata Bazuski alive but unconscious in the back of the van. Her wrists and ankles were bound with duct tape, and another long piece had been stuck across her mouth to keep her from making noise, should she happen to regain her senses. The stink of chloroform hung in the air. It must have been the way he subdued all his victims.

Rosemary removed it right away to make sure it wasn't interfering with her breathing. We got her out of the van, pushing aside brooms and mops and other cleaning stuff, and lowered her gently to the ground. Rosemary freed her hands while I pulled the tape off her ankles.

"You need to go sit down while I call this in," Rosemary said, frowning at me.

"I'm all right." I had a ferocious headache, but my vision was clear and I was steady enough on my feet.

"You've got blood all over you."

I touched my forehead and discovered she was right. The flesh was numb from the force of the blow, but my fingers came away wet and red. I rummaged in the van and found a rag in a bucket. I used it to dab at my forehead. There was more blood down the side of my face and in my beard, and soon the rag was red with it.

As Rosemary walked away, cellphone pressed to her ear, I said, "I'm going in the house."

She waved, waiting for her call to go through.

Pressing the rag to my forehead, I walked toward the verandah. From this angle I could see a small blue car parked at the side of the house. Presumably it was Lucy Banner's car. Hadley must have driven it here to hide it after kidnapping her.

The house was huge, much larger than I'd realized. There was a main building and a wing jutting off to the right. There were three storeys and several balconies, none in very good shape. The verandah wrapped around the house, bordered with a fancy latticework that had somehow withstood the test of time.

The front door was large and heavy-looking, its white paint faded to vanilla. No window. The doorknob was white porcelain in a metal lock piece. I tried it. The door opened. I stepped inside.

The smell hit me first. Rank animal flesh; chemicals; dirt; methane gas.

I found a clean spot on the rag and held it over my nose and mouth.

I'd expected rotten floorboards and collapsed ceilings, but the hallway and front room were in decent shape. The hardwood floors were filthy, though. Cobwebs hung everywhere. There was also garbage—fast food wrappers, empty Coke cups, half-filled trash bags, broken glass. There was no furniture, and nothing hanging on the walls. No paintings, no photographs. Nothing.

I tried a switch and was surprised when lights came

on overhead. The hydro was still connected. If the power was on, then it might be possible that the water was also running. Everything out here was on a well-and-septic system, and if the water pump was working, that would mean the taps were running and the toilets would flush.

I thought that, given the size of this place, there must be a downstairs bathroom, so I went looking for it, hoping to be able to wash the blood from my face and beard. Maybe even look in a mirror to assess the damage. I opened a few doors and stared in at empty rooms.

Finally, I found it.

Or what had once been a washroom. The toilet was still there, iron-stained but reasonably clean, and a small pedestal sink next to it with a cloudy mirror on the wall above it. I didn't take the time to look at myself, though, because the rest of the room caught and held my attention.

The far wall had been torn down to make one large room encompassing the former bathroom and the kitchen. I found a switch and turned on a series of overhead fluorescent lights. The room had been set up as one big workshop for Hadley's taxidermy business.

There were cluttered workbenches and high stools, mounts and stands, pegboards with electric hand tools, several large green garbage pails, and large wooden boxes filled with supplies. I saw a wood-burning kit and blank plaques, plastic containers of doweling in various sizes, and pieces of wood to be used for stands.

The kitchen sink had been replaced by something you might see in an autopsy room, along with a stainless steel dissecting table and overhead magnifiers. Nearby was a small white metal device on wheels. A flume protruded from the top of it and was connected to the chimney where the kitchen wood stove had once been vented out. A metal tag on the side of the thing referred to it as a Floor Sentry fume extractor.

Wall shelves held plastic jugs of tanning chemicals, pickling acid, skin prep bactericide, pre-soaking fluid to protect feathers, fur, and hair, and many other similar products, including the Borax I'd seen Hadley with when he'd punched me in the stomach.

There were assorted animals and a lot of birds. A stuffed Canada Goose hung by wires from the ceiling, its big wings spread out as though in flight. Smaller birds, looking like the ones you'd see along the shoreline of a lake or river, had been mounted on stands and arranged on a shelf by themselves. A big brown owl sat on a table, Hadley's work on it apparently still in progress.

The smell of chemicals was strong in here, and I wondered if Hadley's fume extractor wasn't working properly.

I went out a door into a hallway. In front of me were two large sliding walnut doors. The dining room?

I slid them open.

Nathan Notwell stared out at me with eyes of shining glass.

CHAPTER

Fifty-Five

I backed away from the threshold and threw up on the floor. I bent over, hands on my knees, and kept going until my stomach was empty. As I gasped and spat, a drop of blood ran down my nose and fell into the mess.

I was contaminating a crime scene, I thought dimly, but I had no choice. I had to go into that room. I had to be able to tell Rosemary what had happened to her missing people.

I gathered myself, took several deep breaths, and entered the room.

They were all here, arranged in a tableau intended to resemble a waiting room with couches and a table covered with old magazines. There were five cadavers, all arranged in various poses. In front of each was a stand, like you'd see in a museum, with a plaque explaining the display.

Nathan stood off to one side, with a mop in one hand and a bucket in the other. His plaque read:

> *My name is Billy Marshall. I made fun of Marty when he was learning how to become a good janitor. I tried*

to escape to Halifax but he found me
and made me pay.

Signed, Handsome & very Stupid
Billy.

Sitting alone on a brown leatherette couch was Lucy
Banner, the music teacher. Hadley may have had problems
with her hair, because she was wearing a reddish wig. He'd
arranged her with her knees together and her purse on the
floor beside her foot. The plaque in front of her said:

> *My name is Ruth Muldoon. Whenever*
> *I visited my cousin, Marty's mother,*
> *I treated little Marty like he was the*
> *stupidest person in the universe.*
> *Once I called him a moron that no*
> *one could love, and his mother didn't*
> *say a word to defend him.*
>
> Signed, that smug Bag of Shit
> Ruth.

Standing next to Lucy Banner's couch was Paul Forrest.
He was naked except for a pair of blue gym shorts and
scuffed white sneakers. His plaque said:

> *My name is Johnny Heywood. I made*
> *Marty's life a living hell in Phys Ed. I*
> *humiliated him in the change room*
> *and liked to rabbit punch him in the*
> *back of the head when the teacher*
> *wasn't looking. I'm a foul-smelling*
> *bag of dog vomit with no brain.*
>
> Signed, Johnny the Useless Jock.

The librarian, Emily Clement, was next. She sat in a waiting chair with her hands folded in her lap. Hadley had given her heavy makeup and dressed her in a skimpy green blouse and a short skirt. Her plaque said:

> *My name is Maggie Wilner I lived next door to the Hadleys and babysat Marty. I thought it was hilarious to make fun of his little penis and balls. I fed him spoiled food and slapped him when he threw up. I'm a vicious, foul mouthed piece of shit.*
>
> *Signed, Maggie the Whore.*

The fifth person was unknown to me. He was around the same age as Peter Forrest, and had long red hair that Hadley had combed straight back and sprayed in place. He stood by himself, his arm raised so that he could appear to be looking at his watch. The plaque bore the following inscription:

> *My name is David Thomas. I pretended to be Marty's friend so he'd do my homework for me. To thank him, I started dating the girl he liked and turned her against poor Marty. I got her pregnant and no one ever saw her again.*
>
> *Signed, David the Nasty Prick.*

There was another empty waiting chair in the room with a stand in front of it, but the plaque had not yet been attached. I expected it was probably back in the workshop I'd just left, waiting for its inscription. I felt certain this place had been prepared for Renata Bazuski.

It was a room from hell. It smelled of formaldehyde, mildewed clothing, and mouse urine. The depravity of the mind that had been capable of committing this horrifying atrocity staggered the imagination. Hadley's evil was overwhelming.

I felt like I couldn't breathe.

Stumbling out of the room, I fled the house and, once outside, fell to my knees on the ground. As I retched in painful dry heaves, the paramedics arrived to tend to Renata Bazuski.

EPILOGUE

Six Months Later

Today was a good day.

This afternoon I put the finishing touches to a rough of my first single-panel gag since last August. It shows two dogs sitting at a bar. Their ties are loosened and they both have water bowls in front of them. The first dog says, "I couldn't help noticing you're wearing a red sock and a blue sock." The other dog replies, "I know. And I've got another pair at home just like them."

The joke is so old that Egyptologists must have transcribed it from the hieroglyphs, and it combines two well-worn tropes—dogs acting like people, and two guys sitting at a bar—but I took it all the way from a quick sketch to a submissible rough without abandoning it while still only half done—something I haven't been able to do for quite a while—so I was pleased with it.

Into the files it went.

It's been a difficult winter.

Turning seventy ended up being the least of my problems. Stumbling onto Martin Hadley's horror tableau, as it happened, was traumatic for me in the extreme, and I needed therapy over the next while to work my way through it, to learn how to sleep at night again without medication, and to return my focus to the world around me rather than the scorched landscape within.

Unable to draw or write things that were humorous, amusing, or light-spirited, I turned my attention elsewhere.

The police, the labs, the Crown, and the Coroner's Office descended on the abandoned house on Muldoon Side Road with all the resources at their disposal. The physical evidence they collected was more than enough to put Martin Hadley away for five lifetimes. Perversely, however, he insisted on pleading not guilty, and a trial was held in which Patrick, Rosemary, and I were all compelled to testify. It was extremely unpleasant, to say the least.

I found out that the fifth victim was a young man named Gary Shea, who'd gone missing from his home in Drummond Township several months before Emily Clement, making him the first of Hadley's victims. His mother had assumed he'd left on his own, and had never bothered to call police. Apparently she'd been afraid that they'd discover the meth lab being operated in their barn by Gary's older brother, Dwight.

One thing that had finally become clear to me is that the reason we hadn't been able to find concrete connections among the victims, other than the noisy van, was that there were none outside of the tormented mind of Martin Hadley. It would seem that in plotting his revenge on various people who'd wronged him in his life, all of whom were in reality out of his reach for one reason or another, he'd waited until someone appeared on his radar who resembled them before hunting them down and killing them for his tableau. Nathan reminded him of Billy Marshall, Mrs. Banner reminded him of Ruth Muldoon, and so on. It made me feel slightly better—only slightly, of course—to know that we hadn't been overlooking obvious links among the real victims because we were too stupid or inexperienced to detect them. They simply didn't exist.

A side benefit of Mrs. Hadley's stubborn insistence on her son fighting the charges was that she was forced to sell off property she owned in order to pay for dear Marty's high-profile criminal defence attorney. As it happened, the property on Muldoon Side Road being used by her son as a horror sideshow belonged to her. It had passed to her from her late husband, Robert John Hadley, a middle manager with Canadian Pacific Railway. His maternal grandfather, John Parnell Muldoon, had been a senior executive with CPR and had built the house when Edward was still king of England. At the time, it was a veritable mansion, but by the time it had passed down to Mrs. Hadley, it had been abandoned for more than thirty years and was waiting to be torn down.

When I heard Mrs. Hadley was going to put the property on the market—the house and twelve acres of land—I arranged for my lawyer to purchase it for me. Of course, if she'd known she was selling it to me she would have refused, despite her urgent need of funds. As it was, though, we were able to engineer the thing so that the deed passed into my hands with no fuss at all. At a price below its value.

I immediately inquired about having the house demolished, but my lawyer explained it couldn't be done until the trial was over because it remained a crime scene and still contained physical evidence relevant to the legal process that was underway. I was discouraged, because the

Hadleys were sending clear messages that they'd appeal any decision not in their favour, but after he was convicted on all counts and sentenced to consecutive life sentences there was no more money and, after all their bluster, there were no appeals.

As soon as I heard the news, I got on the phone to begin arrangements to have the house torn down in the spring.

I hadn't waited to make other changes to the property, though. As soon as the sale cleared and the land belonged to me, I directed my lawyer to put in motion the required steps to amend the zoning to allow for Rosemary's house trailer. I arranged with the township to create an entrance to the lot off the short stretch facing on Tennyson Road, and I scheduled a landscaping company to clear a spot for her when the snow was gone, with enough room for a lawn, a garden, a shelter for her bike, and whatever else might cross her mind.

While accommodating as many of the oak trees as possible, of course. For my sake.

When Rosemary's deadline arrived to remove her trailer from her cousin's property last fall, we had it brought here to my place, where it stayed for the winter while Rosemary moved into my guest bedroom. Which lasted for about a month.

At which point she moved in with Patrick, and *that* whole thing began to take shape.

Tell me you saw it coming. Hmm?

Next month I'll get a well drilled and arrange for the hydro hook-up, after which we'll move the Airstream over to its new location. Rosemary plans to move in, although it's my impression that intensive talks are underway with Patrick as to future living arrangements. Whatever they decide will suit me. The trailer will be here, waiting.

What else?

Oh, yes. My new book, *They Just Don't Get It, Do They?*, will release next month. Perrin Olsen and Meg Bantree have arranged for a big launch in London and, like a fool, I agreed to attend.

Darlene is excited to go with me. She's disappointed she can't bring Buzzy, but as I said to her, "Mrs. Leahy, please remember that two's company and three's a crowd. Besides, Sabrina can't go either."

She relented, smiling that sweet smile of hers.

What? You didn't think I'd let that opportunity slip past me, did you?

Which is pretty much a wrap.

I'm reminded of a cartoon by a late friend of mine, Lo Linkert. Lo was a German paratrooper in World War Two who ended up in a hospital in a Canadian prisoner-of-war camp. He and his wife moved to Canada after the war, and he set about building a career the hard way, one cartoon at a time. He specialized in golf cartoons and naked women gags, but the one I remember best is a tried-and-true desert island cartoon featuring two stranded men staring at the distant horizon, which consists of a dotted line. Above it are the words: "TEAR ALONG THIS LINE."

The one guy looks at the other and says, "I'm game if you are."

Seventy's just a number. I've got a lot of stuff to do, so, Hell yeah, I'm game.

Let's get busy.

Fin

Acknowledgments

Once again, it's important to note that this novel is a work of fiction. Characters and events are entirely the invention of the author. All resemblances to actual people or occurrences are strictly coincidental.

All single-panel gag descriptions attributed to Mark Heron have been fabricated by the author. Descriptions of actual gags by actual cartoonists are noted in the text as such.

Rosemary's possum T-shirt is the creation of a small company called Shirtmandude, Fun Shirts for Weird People, which designs original graphics and prints them by hand onto tees. They're available from shirtmandude.com. I couldn't resist quoting this one, and I hope the company doesn't mind.

The following publications were helpful in the writing of this novel: Roy Paul Nelson, *Cartooning* (Chicago: Henry Regnery Company, 1975); Bill Mauldin, *Up Front* (New York: Henry Holt and Company, 1945); Marvin Rosenberg and William Cole, eds., *The Best Cartoons from Punch* (New York: Simon and Schuster, 1952); and Peter Arno, *Peter Arno's Ladies and Gentlemen* (New York: Simon and Schuster, 1951).

The anecdote regarding Bill Lee was found online: Steven Heller, "The Daily Heller: When Art is Garbage." *Print*, April 11, 2022, printmag.com/daily-heller/the-daily-heller-unintentional street-art/, viewed July 27, 2023.

Thanks as always to my editor and life partner, the fabulous Lynn L. Clark.

About the Author

Michael J. McCann lives and writes in Oxford Station, Ontario, Canada. A graduate of Trent University (Peterborough, ON) and Queen's University (Kingston, ON), he served as Production Editor of *Criminal Reports (Third Series)* and Law Reports Co-ordinator for Carswell Legal Publications (Western) before spending fifteen years at the Canada Border Services Agency as a project officer and national program manager. He's married to author Lynn L. Clark. They have one son.

If you enjoyed this crime novel,
you'll also love the debut of
retired detective Tom Faust in

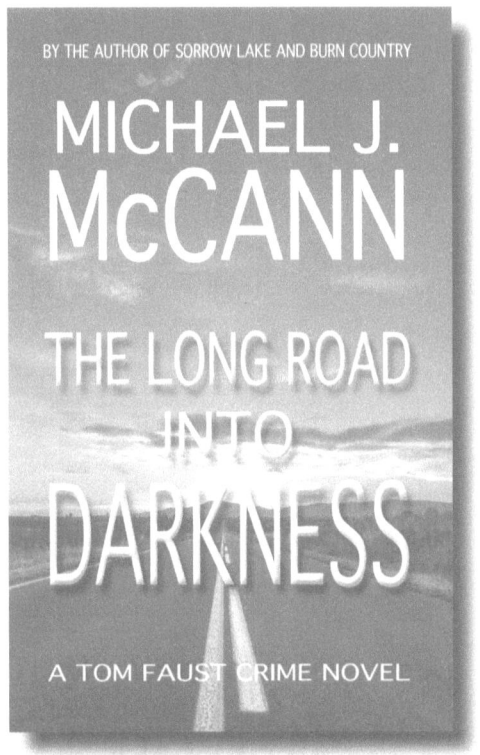

BY THE AUTHOR OF SORROW LAKE AND BURN COUNTRY

MICHAEL J.
McCANN

THE LONG ROAD
INTO
DARKNESS

A TOM FAUST CRIME NOVEL

The Long Road Into Darkness
Michael J. McCann
ISBN: 978-1-927884-17-1

**Ask your local independent bookstore
to order it today!**

Finalist for the
HAMMETT PRIZE
Best Crime Novel in North America

BY THE AUTHOR OF THE DONAGHUE AND STAINER CRIME NOVEL SERIES

MICHAEL J. McCANN

SORROW LAKE

"McCann has a convincing way with character and plot."
—Toronto Star

A MARCH AND WALKER CRIME NOVEL

Sorrow Lake
March and Walker #1
Michael J. McCann
ISBN: 978-1-927884-02-7

Ask your local independent bookstore
to order it today!

**Maddie Hubbard must face
her greatest fears
before they drive her mad.**

**Twilight Road
A Maddie Hubbard Novel**
Michael J. McCann
ISBN: 978-1-927884-23-2

**Ask your local independent bookstore
to order it today!**

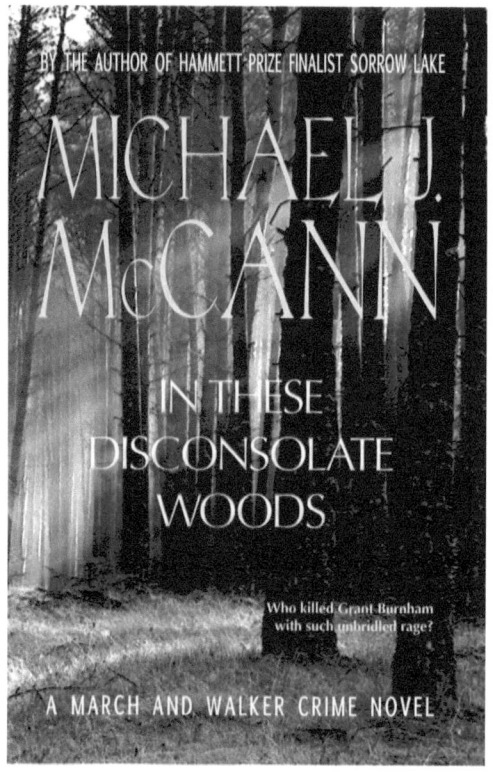

www.ingramcontent.com/pod-product-compliance
Lightning Source LLC
Chambersburg PA
CBHW020648030726
47498CB00002B/418